BROKEN SKY

STONE BAY SERIES PREQUEL

PERSEPHONE AUTUMN

BETWEEN WORDS PUBLISHING LLC

Broken Sky

Copyright © 2022 by Persephone Autumn

www.persephoneautumn.com

ISBN: 978-1-951477-34-9 (Ebook)

ISBN: 978-1-951477-35-6 (Paperback)

Editor: Ellie McLove | My Brother's Editor

Proofreader: Rosa Sharon | My Brother's Editor

Cover Design: Abigail Davies | Pink Elephant Designs

To all the wonderful readers that keep picking up my books… I love you!
Thank you for your continued support, but most of all your friendship 🖤

BOOKS BY PERSEPHONE AUTUMN

Bay Area Duet Series

Click Duet

Through the Lens

Time Exposure

Inked Duet

Fine Line

Love Buzz

Insomniac Duet

Restless Night

A Love So Bright

Artist Duet

Blank Canvas

Abstract Passion

Lake Lavender Series

Depths Awakened

One Night Forsaken

Every Thought Taken

Stone Bay Series

Broken Sky: Stone Bay Series Prequel

Devotion Series

Distorted Devotion

Undying Devotion

Beloved Devotion

Darkest Devotion

Sweetest Devotion

Standalone Romance Novels

Sweet Tooth

Transcendental

Poetry Collections

Ink Veins

Broken Metronome

Published Under P. Autumn

Standalone Horror Novels

By Dawn

ONE

SKYLAR

"HE'S LOOKING AT YOU AGAIN," Kirsten says in my ear.

I lift the brown bottle to my lips, take a sip, and peer down the bar. For the third time, the man at the end has his eyes locked on my profile. Before he catches my stare, I avert my gaze to the wall of liquor bottles. Study the colored glass with too much interest.

"Can we go?" I twist to face Kirsten. "Please."

Coming out to the bar was not my idea. Personally, I'd rather sit on the couch with sour cream and onion potato chips, red licorice, chocolate, and a can of Dr Pepper. Binge-watch true crime documentaries all night with the lights off and curtains drawn.

Sounds like heaven.

Unlike these constricting heels Kirsten insisted I wear tonight. Along with the skintight, leaves-nothing-to-the-imagination red dress. Both of which came from her closet. Not that I wouldn't own them, but I tend to lean toward nonconstrictive apparel and flatter shoes.

Kirsten pushes out her bottom lip and tilts her head. "But we haven't danced yet."

Dancing and I are not best friends. Kirsten is well aware of this fact. If she wasn't already on her second Long Island Iced Tea, she would remember this. And I would probably say no. But then she sticks her lower lip out farther and bounces like a child ready to throw a hissy fit.

So, like the good friend I am, I cave.

"Fine." She smiles and claps and bounces for a different reason. I hold a finger up and point at her. "But only for a few minutes. Then, I'm leaving."

"You're like an old lady. It's not even midnight." I cock a brow and she raises her hands in surrender. "But I'll take what I can get. Sheesh."

I drink the last of my beer before she drags me onto the dance floor. Literally. I almost face-plant from these ridiculous heels.

One dance, then I can kick these heels off.

Dead center in Dalton's Pub and Billiards, with maybe thirty other people on the open dance floor space, Kirsten throws her hands in the air, tips her head back, and swings her hips to the music. My skin dampens as I join in. My eyes dart around the crowd, making a mental note of everyone here. I love to dance, but prefer to embarrass myself in privacy.

Thankfully, I know no one here tonight.

Live a little, Sky. You're young, vivacious, and gorgeous. That is what everyone tells me, anyway.

The pub music varies from song to song, depending on who gets to the jukebox first. At the moment, a pop song from early last year spills from hidden speakers. I close my eyes for two deep breaths, then sway to the beat. One song transitions into another and I get lost in the music. Forget about my dislike of crowds, my phobia of being the center of attention, and enjoy the night out.

When my eyes reopen, Kirsten's widen as they look over my shoulder. Before I open my mouth to ask what is wrong, a wall of heat blankets my backside. Whoever it is, they aren't so close we touch. Our bodies inches apart. A stranger standing far too close. An invasion of my private bubble.

I mouth to Kirsten, "Is it him?"

Imperceptibly, she nods.

Great.

Somehow, some unfamiliar instinct deep down knew it was him.

My eyes close for one deep breath before I spin to face the man from the end of the bar. Ask him why he kept staring my way. Why he followed me to the dance floor. In the process, and because grace is not my middle name, I twist my ankle and fall forward. On him.

Fuck. My. Life.

"Are you okay?" he shouts above the music, hands cupping my elbows.

I peer up to the man that not only caused the problem

but saved me from face-planting on the hardwood. Thank you is on the tip of my tongue, ready to spill from my lips, but my mouth refuses to open. Instead, I gawk at the man. Stare into his shimmering brown irises and lose all train of thought.

Who am I right now?

Straightening my spine, pain shoots up my leg as I add weight to the injured ankle. "Shit!" I lift my foot and reach for his bicep. "Ow, ow, ow."

Tall Mature and Mysterious shifts his weight, snakes an arm around my waist, and practically carries me off the dance floor. Instinct screams at me to protest his help, rip his arm off me, and hobble to a chair on my own. I don't know this man, don't know if he's some creeper who preys on younger women, then murders them on desolate highways.

Stone Bay has its share of dark back roads. Plenty of places for people to go missing.

That said, I cling to him. Curl my fingers tighter around his bicep. Salivate over the girth beneath his sleeve. Tell instinct to shut it while attraction works her magic. Because this man has definitely been conjured by the gods.

He parks me on a stool and drops his hand from my waist. My lower lip pops out for one, two, three heartbeats before my lips part and I gasp. The semicoherence I gained from sitting is stolen by Mr. Magic as his hand drifts down my hip, along the outside of my thigh. His nails gingerly bite my skin as he passes the hem of my dress and slides down, down, down to my ankle. My thighs clamp together and a wicked smile dons his face.

"Should take these off."

His words drift past me as I stare at him. "Sorry, what?"

My leg is cradled in one of his hands while he caresses my ankle with the other. "The shoes. You should take them off."

Oh. Right. The shoes. I curse whoever made these heels — probably a man — then thank him. Without them, I wouldn't be in this predicament.

"Uh..." I bite my bottom lip as the man remains crouched at my feet. "I don't have anything else to wear." And there is no way in hell I am walking barefoot in this bar. Or any bar, for that matter. Who the hell knows what is on the floor.

As if he senses my dilemma, he rises and steps forward, wedging one leg between mine as he cages me in with his arms on the stool back. My pulse doubles and breath quickens as his stubbled jaw grazes my cheek. Breath hot on my ear.

"I'll carry you."

Oh, I bet you will.

When I don't answer him, he leans back enough to make eye contact. A breath between us, I silently beg for his lips. Anywhere. Everywhere.

What is it about him that has me compromising every boundary, every ounce of self-preservation? I would shove aside any other man. Tell them I don't *need* their help.

Declare my independence as a woman. But minutes with this guy and my brain goes rubbery.

"Thanks for the offer." I inch forward, a silent signal I want to stand, but the man doesn't budge. "Do you mind?" Pointing past him, I indicate my desire to leave.

And once again, he stands his ground. Alarms and flashing lights should be going off in my head. Red flags should be flying high everywhere I look.

Obviously, my internal security system is malfunctioning.

"You're in no shape to walk. Allow me to help. Please."

Where the hell is Kirsten?

I peer around Mr. Magic and spot my friend, her ass grinding against an anonymous groin. Which means girls' night is officially over. No doubt she assumes I plan to go home with the man ogling me the last hour. Wouldn't be the first time we came to the pub together and left separately.

Tonight feels different, though. *He* is different. Older. Darker. Edgier.

He makes my pulse pound and breath stutter. Equal parts desire and fear.

How many times have I picked up a guy in the pub? More than I can count on one hand. Not saying I'm easy, but I enjoy life. Do what I want. And if one of those things happens to be sex with strangers, so be it. If guys get to hook up with whoever they please and not be judged, so can I. But the guys of the past were a little softer around the edges. Quieter. Kind of like me until I get to know someone.

"Fine," I huff out as my eyes come back to his. The corners of his mouth and eyes perk up. "But" —I hold up a finger— "what's your name?"

"Law."

"Law?" He cocks a brow and nods. "What kind of name is *Law*? Your parents work in criminal justice or something?"

It's a joke. A way for me to lighten the mood. But it does nothing of the sort. Instead, he steps into me and purses his lips as his eyes shift left, then right, then left again.

My shoulders plummet. I open my mouth to apologize, but as the words of regret form on my tongue, all the seriousness vanishes from his face. In its place is the biggest smile. His entire frame shakes. Before I comprehend what is happening, laughter rips from his lips.

"Sorry." More laughter. "It's really not that funny." He clutches his stomach with one hand and presses a closed fist to his lips with the other. "Guess it's funnier in my head."

"What?" I ask, irritated that he continues to laugh when I thought I had offended him.

"I was going to give some phony sad story, but you're too fucking adorable."

"Huh?"

"Lawrence. Law is short for Lawrence."

"What a sophisticated name."

He steps closer, warming my skin with his. "And what's your name?"

I swallow and trace the sharp line of his jaw with my eyes. Lick my lips and envision the scruff between my legs, chafing my thighs.

"Sky. Skylar," I stammer.

"Well, Sky, Skylar, what do you say we get you home and off your feet?"

I shake my head and nod simultaneously. No doubt I look like a fool, with my head jittering in every direction. But Law doesn't seem to care one bit. Matter of fact, he appears rather amused by my flustered state.

Can't help it, though. The man has charisma unlike any I have seen before. Maybe it's his maturity. Perhaps his confidence. Either way, I want everything he has to offer.

"Yeah, sounds good."

Know what else sounds good? Going to his place and not mine. Time to work some magic of my own.

TWO

LAWRENCE

"DID YOU DRIVE?"

Skylar shakes her head. "We don't get behind the wheel on pub nights."

Pub nights.

The two words roll off her tongue with ease. How often do pub nights happen? Better yet, how often does she leave the pub with random men?

Don't ask questions you don't want the answer to, Law.

"Good." I steer us toward my car, one arm around her waist, her hand hooked on my shoulder. Her shoes dangle from the other hand. "Sure you're okay with me driving you home?"

Her grip on me tightens as she clamps down on her lips and scrunches her eyes. A muffled hiss spills from her lips. She must have stepped wrong. Put too much weight on her ankle. Pain evident in the pinch of her brow and shift in her weight.

It's tempting to stop us. To whisk her up in my arms and carry her to the car. Frail as Skylar is with a sprained ankle, she gives off independent woman vibes. A woman of quiet strength.

"Unless you want to drive me to *your* home." The pain on her face seconds ago is replaced with mischief.

Would I like Skylar in my house, my space, my bed? Damn straight. Anyone who found her attractive would. But I don't want to be another random guy to her.

We reach the car and I grip the door handle to unlock it. I help lower her into the seat, shut the door, then jog to the driver's side. I press the ignition, crank the air conditioning, then twist in my seat.

"Tempting, but it's probably best to be in your own space with that injury."

Her bottom lip pushes out in the cutest fucking pout. A pout with a direct connection to my groin. I bite the inside of my cheek and stifle the groan in my throat.

"Fine," she huffs out. "I'm not far from the Trading Post, on Jasper."

Nice neighborhood. I study her profile, her clothes, the way she carries herself. She doesn't appear snobbish or spoiled. No, Skylar looks like a hardworking woman. A woman who doesn't take handouts without paying it forward. The skintight dress hugs her curves as if made for her, but I have a sneaking suspicion it doesn't normally hang in her closet.

Skylar may have nice things and live in a mid-class neighborhood, but I bet she busted her ass for all of it.

I steer the car out of the lot and drive away from the center of town.

Stone Bay, Washington, isn't big by any means, but sizable enough to have a spot on the map and attract tourists. Visitors boost the town's revenue, but we don't depend on them. Generations of old money reside in the roots of Stone Bay. Some flaunt their inheritance, like town royalty. But plenty live an average existence, spending only what is necessary to live.

"So, Skylar..." I glance to the passenger seat as she shivers. "Are you cold?" She shakes her head, but I adjust the air anyway. "Tell me about you."

She shifts in her seat, knees bumping the center console. "What do you want to know?"

Everything. "Whatever you want to share." I shrug, my eyes back on the road.

From the corner of my eye, I notice her fingers fidget in her lap. Her right thumb and forefinger twisting a ring on her left thumb. Do I make her uncomfortable? Odd, considering she willingly left the pub with me and got in my car. Hell, she flirted and suggested going to my place.

"Um..." She breaks her hands apart and pins them between her thighs and the seat. "Not much to tell." She laughs without humor. "My life's pretty boring. Tonight" —she points over her shoulder—"at the pub, that's about as wild as my nights get."

We must have varying definitions of wild. In my early twenties, I spent most nights at the pub or parties. Drank enough to wake up with a grueling headache and no memory of what or who I did the night before. Didn't take long before those nights ended. Fun as they were, graduating with a finance degree superseded the need to party.

"How often are these wild nights?"

Am I an asshole for asking how often she drinks and leaves with other men? Or am I an asshole for assuming every time she goes out to drink, she leaves with men? Either way, I am an asshole.

"Do I sense a hint of jealousy?"

There is the flirty woman I eyed from the end of the bar. Skylar may be somewhat reserved, but I sense the silent vixen living inside her. No way a woman with phoenix-red curls can be wholly docile. No, she has fire in her veins.

"Maybe."

She hums. "Not often. Once every couple of months. I'd rather watch documentaries in the dark with junk food." Laughter bubbles in my chest and escapes my lips. Skylar smacks my bicep. "Didn't anyone teach you it's not nice to laugh at the expense of others?"

This makes me laugh harder. "Sorry." I stifle my laughter. "Just hard to picture you eating candy and watching nature shows."

"Who says I watch nature?" she challenges. I turn onto Jasper and she points to the left. "Gray house with the silver SUV."

I pull in behind the SUV and throw the car in park. "No whales and rain forests?"

She shakes her head and laughs. "No. More like Bundy and Manson and Dahmer."

My brows shoot to my hairline. "Well... I'd thought about joining you inside. Not sure that's a good idea now."

Skylar unbuckles her belt and twists to face me fully, her lips turned up in amusement. "You're not scared of little old me, are you?" Her tone is teasing. One brow cocked as she licks her lips.

No, little phoenix. It'll take a hell of a lot more to scare me.

I reach across the console and twirl a lock of her hair around my finger. Toy with the curls. Her breath catches. Body leans forward. Tongue darts out to lick her lips. I've not touched her, yet her body begs for more. For my hands on her skin, in her hair, kneading and tugging and teasing. For my mouth on her lips, her neck, and the curves of her body.

And I love how amped up I have her. How easily I could bend her to my will. If I wanted. Lucky for her—or maybe not so lucky—I am not one to take advantage. No, I like to take my time. Treasure my gifts. Peel away the gift wrap and enjoy the anticipation.

The corner of my mouth kicks up. "No, I'm not scared of you." Her shoulders drop as she harrumphs. "But I'm utterly fascinated," I admit.

She toys with the thin silver band on her thumb again. "Would you like to come in?" She tips her head toward the house.

Now I get her nerves. Not sure what Skylar expects if I follow her inside. Maybe she has no expectations.

Maybe she is simply being cordial because I drove her home. Or maybe her invitation has a well-defined answer. No matter, I will at least walk her to the door. Make sure she doesn't injure herself further.

But that is it.

Fiery as Skylar is, tonight should end at her doorstep. Stepping foot in her home is a bad idea. How old is she? Old enough to drink at a bar. Old enough to stir libidinous thoughts. Old enough to lie beneath me.

I should decline her invitation. Should walk her to the door, then drive home. Home to my bed, where I can explore my lewd thoughts with a tight grip on my cock.

I should leave, but I don't.

"I'd love to, thanks."

THREE

SKYLAR

LAWRENCE SWALLOWS the foyer with his presence. Not with his height or stance, but with his aura. He radiates confidence. Projects it like a weapon.

It's pretty hot.

Most guys I have gone home with were handsy the moment we left the pub until I escaped their bed. Which was fine by me. Both of us got what we wanted and called it a night.

But Lawrence didn't seem like most guys.

One—he is older than the men I usually hook up with. How old? Not sure. Guessing age isn't my area of expertise. But if his maturity and sense of self are any indication, I would guess he has at least ten years on me. Two— he dresses sharper, classier. Makes jeans and a pressed, untucked button-down hot.

I hang my purse on a hook near the door, drop the evil

heels on the floor, and hobble farther into the house. "Can I get you water? Dr Pepper?"

His eyes scan the space, take in the blended tastes of me, Kirsten, and our other roommate, Delilah. Thankfully, we have similar taste. Soft neutrals mixed with dark bolds. Basic furniture and simple accent pieces. Considering how busy we are with work and life, we didn't see the point in excess.

"No, thank you. Why don't you sit and I'll get ice for your ankle."

"It's fine —"

Lawrence sweeps me into his arms and walks me to the couch. He lowers me as if I might break. "Sit here. I'll be back."

Okay, then. Lawrence is the bossy type. Should I be surprised? Probably not.

I peek over my shoulder, spot him rummaging through drawers until he locates the gallon zip bags. He opens the freezer, fills the bag with ice, then tugs the towel off the oven door and heads back to the living room.

"What is it you do for work?" I ask as he kneels in front of me, sits, then lifts my ankle to rest it on his knee.

He wraps the towel around the ice before draping the pack over my ankle. Within seconds, the chill alleviates some of the pain. I sag back on the couch and hug a throw pillow to my chest as Lawrence rubs the muscles above my ankle.

Damn, that feels good.

"Investments," he says with a straighter spine and hint

of a smile. "Been with Stone Bay Financial fifteen years." I choke on the air I breathe. Toss the pillow aside, sit upright, and smack my chest. Lawrence gingerly sets my foot on the floor, rises to his knees, and rubs my back. "Lift your hands over your head. Do you want water?"

I lift my arms and shake my head. "I'm okay," I choke out.

Jesus. This man started his career when I was in third grade.

One after another, I take deep breaths. Get my coughing under control. Work to settle the whirlwind of thoughts in my head.

He can't be that *old. Right?*

"Sure you're okay?" He rocks back on his haunches and studies my expression. No doubt my face is beet red.

I nod. "Yeah. Better now." I close my eyes, swallow to dampen my throat, then ask, "How old are you?" My eyes meet his for one, two, three breaths before a hint of a smile dons his lips.

"Is that what made you nearly choke to death?"

I roll my eyes. "It was a dry spot." I tap my throat.

He resumes his spot on the floor, picking up my foot and setting it on his knee again. "Sure it was." He chuckles. "Does it matter how old I am?"

No. Based on appearance, Lawrence has aged well. I don't know much about the financial industry, but if he has been in it fifteen years, I assume he is in his early to midthirties at minimum.

"Not really."

His hand massages near my ankle again and I melt

into the couch. "Thirty-nine." I stiffen and his hand stops. "Relax, Skylar. I'm not some creepy pervert," he teases. My limbs loosen, the rest of my body following suit. "Yes, I'm older." He cocks a brow. "That shouldn't matter." The hand massaging my lower calf inches up closer to my knee. "Tell me it doesn't matter."

"It doesn't matter," I say without hesitation.

A wicked half smile accents his stubble. His hand glides past my knee and works the muscles at the base of my thigh. "Tell me, Skylar. How old are you?"

Sweat dampens my skin as Lawrence holds my gaze and kneads my thigh. Ache builds between my legs. Hunger. Want. To clench my thighs and add friction where I need it most. I silently beg him to inch his palm higher. Run his finger over my swollen clit and slick folds. Quench the thirst building in my core.

But he doesn't heed my silent cries.

"Twenty-three," I answer, breathy.

His hand slides back down my leg. Before I protest, he removes the ice, lifts my ankle to his lips, and kisses the inside of the joint. "Better?"

My ankle? No clue. All I can focus on right now is his lips on my skin. On the heat no ice pack will dull.

I nod. "Mmmhmm." I would embellish, but fear I will choke on my words.

He kisses the inside of my ankle again, his hand kneading up my calf once more. "You sure?" His lips follow the path of his hand as he hooks my ankle over his shoulder. One hand locks my leg to his shoulder while the other trails up, up, up my thigh.

Instinctually, I part my legs. Grant him permission to travel beneath the hem of my dress, to the lace of my panties. The skirt shifts higher, exposes a hint of what is to come. He groans against my skin. Nips the inside of my knee as his hand inches the dress higher. Spreads my legs wider as his tongue licks closer to my panties.

Then he stops. His mouth a breath from my center. The tip of his nose grazing the thin elastic band of my panties. He hovers and I forget how to breathe.

He doesn't move. His breath hot on my lace-covered, bare mound. "Tell me to stop."

My fingers comb through his thick, black strands, curl into a fist, and jerk his head back until our eyes meet. "Never."

He growls. The muscles in his jaw flex. "Fuck, you smell like heaven."

I lick my lips and hold his gaze. "Bet I taste like it too."

"Jesus," he grits out. His hands crawl up my thighs to the band of my panties, slowly peeling them down and off. He throws my other leg over his shoulder, scoops under my ass, and says, "Hold on."

Before I register what he said, he scoots me to the edge of the couch, the dress riding up and over my hips. The tip of his nose runs up my slick seam and pauses just above my clit. He inhales deeply and kneads my hips. Then he licks up my center. Moans when he reaches my clit. Drags my hips closer and buries his mouth between my thighs.

Sweet mother of all things holy.

I fist his hair and the couch cushion. Dig my heels into his back and grind against his talented tongue. I release his hair, grab the hem of the dress, and tug it over my head. Unfasten my bra and free my breasts.

He tears his mouth away and rakes his eyes up my exposed flesh. "You're a fucking dream, little phoenix. A dream I never want to end."

"Take your shirt off," I tell him. One by one, he unfastens the buttons and tosses the shirt aside. His tanned skin highlighted with tribal patterns on one arm. Something I will study later. Now, I have other priorities. "Lie on the floor."

"Demanding," he teases as he lies back.

"Only when I know what I want."

"I'll remember that."

I straddle his face. "Best you do."

He palms my ass as I lower myself. His tongue darting out and tasting me once more. I rock my hips back and forth, over and over, as I pinch my nipples.

Stubble digs into my thighs and the sensitive flesh between my legs as I grind harder, faster. One of his hands shifts, slides down my ass crack, passes the tight hole, and dips inside my pussy.

"Yes," I moan, tipping my head back.

He inserts another digit. Has me riding his hand and face with urgency. I drop a hand from my breast, reach back and palm his cock through the denim. His growl of appreciation adds a delicious vibration as he pumps his fingers faster. I unbutton his jeans, slide down the zipper, and shove my hand in his briefs. I fuck his face and jerk his cock in a vicious rhythm.

Reaching up, he pinches my nipple. Hard. Adds a little teeth to my clit. I jerk him harder. Circle my hips and add more pressure. Quicken my pace as my orgasm builds. And then, I free-fall. Lawrence brings his hands to my ass and locks me in place. Devours me until I come back down.

Dropping my hands to the rug, I slowly rise off Lawrence and regulate my breathing. Crawl up the couch, fetch the throw blanket, and wrap it around my body.

"Mind if I use the bathroom?" he asks, standing and adjusting himself.

"Not at all." I bite my lip. "I should finish you, too."

He grips my chin and tips my head back to meet his gaze. "Another time."

I stick out my bottom lip. "Okay."

Rising from the couch, I collect the dress and my undergarments while he fetches his shirt, then show him to the bathroom. While he cleans up, I ditch the blanket and put on my robe.

We meet in the hall, him dressed like nothing happened and me bare beneath silk.

"I should head out," he says. My shoulders slump before I cross my arms over my chest. "Hey." He tips my chin back so I meet his stare. "Your pouting is cute, but please don't." I tuck my lips between my teeth and nod. "Can I see you again?"

My lips free themselves and curve up at the corners. "Yes."

He pulls his phone from his back pocket, unlocks it, and hands it to me. Behind the apps is a generic background, probably one that comes with the phone. "Will you add your contact info?"

I nod and enter my details. Before I hand it back, I open his messaging app and send myself a text.

For the first time ever, I don't want to spend the night alone. But I know nothing about this man. Nothing except what happened since we left the pub. I want him to stay, but know he should leave.

The walk to the front door is slow and quiet. Like a walk of shame with no witnesses. I reach for the knob, but he swoops in before I make contact. Cradles my hand in his.

"What's wrong, Skylar?"

Ugh. I hate this. Hate the sudden vulnerability coursing through my veins. Hate the heat on my cheeks and uncertainty of meeting his eyes.

Despite what I feel, I look up and find no humor or deceit or malice in his expression. I take a deep breath and shake my head.

"Nothing. Just don't do well with goodbyes." Half-truth. I have never had a problem saying goodbye to guys. It's family I have a tougher time with.

He leans in and kisses my forehead. "Only goodbye for now." I nod and he drops my hand, reaches for the handle and twists. He steps outside and I follow. Spinning to face me, he brings his hands to my cheeks. "Glad to have met you, Skylar." His lips collide with mine, my taste still on his tongue. "See you soon."

"See you."

And then he strolls to his car, hops in, and drives away.

FOUR

LAWRENCE

"YOU WITH US, LAW?"

Locking my phone, I set it on the conference table and look to Garrett. "Yeah, sorry."

Am I though? Not really.

Skylar sent me a selfie of her wearing white shorts that made her legs a mile long and a dark green, off the shoulder, bohemian top. The green pops against her fiery curls and adds a layer of confidence to her light eyes. I couldn't look away or fight the bulge beneath my zipper.

Since the night at Skylar's house two weeks back, she has taken up residence in every waking thought. That night, her response to my mouth, my touch... Skylar is a damn siren. A firestorm waiting for the wind to set her ablaze. And I want to watch her burn fiercely. Preferably beneath me. Above works too.

Much to the disagreement of my nearly constant erection, there is also no need to rush. Although she harnessed bravery like a sword in privacy, Skylar didn't want to be the center of attention in public. Her banter and wit are adorable, but nonetheless a disguise. A way to shelter her bashful side from the masses. A method of protection.

I want more of her meekness, though. Something about her natural reservation turns me on. It is what had my eyes glued to her in the pub. What pushed me to pursue her.

"Proposal for the Hughes account should be ready tomorrow. Have you reached out to the Barron's about updating their beneficiaries?" Terrance asks. "Heard another heir arrived last week." A hint of sarcasm in his tone.

"Scheduled to call them in the morning," I answer.

The Barrons—one of the original families in Stone Bay. Seven families the town put on a pedestal decades ago. Too bad not all those families are as respectable as they once were. Ego and greed change people. I learned this firsthand.

"Great. Keep us posted. What's on your docket?" Terrance turns to Garrett.

"Touching base with the banks for more prospects."

Strictly an investment firm, Stone Bay Financial didn't handle the day-to-day finances of the townsfolk. We left that to the two small banks in town. Both offer savings options, but deposit certificates didn't appeal to everyone. The banks also weren't equipped to handle our clients' wealth. Once a week, we visit the banks and talk prospects with the staff. For every new client we attain, we share the wealth (in the form of new accounts) with the office. Everyone wins.

"With summer right around the corner, I'm following up with clients who have vacation properties and investment homes. Updating assets while probing for new opportunities," Terrance shares.

We jot down notes on yellow legal pads and review our individual talking points before the meeting ends.

"Anything else?" Garrett asks. Terrance and I shake our heads. "Great. Now on to the best part of the meeting." He pins me with a stare. "What's up with you?"

My brows pinch at the middle. "Not sure what you mean."

"No offense, but I've never seen you happier. What changed?"

Garrett and Terrance are more than coworkers. More than people I talk business with. Over the years, we developed a solid friendship. A bond that rivals the one I share with my brother. In our line of business, trust matters. It is only natural for it to transfer to our personal lives too.

Although I trust Terrance and Garrett with my life, a voice in the back of my head says not to mention Skylar. Not yet.

It's not embarrassment or the fear of judgment setting off warning bells. Something just isn't *right*, and it has nothing to do with Skylar. The strange twist of instinct has me uneasy. On edge. If only I knew the reason why.

I ponder over a list of generic answers and pick the one that seems least obvious and questionable. "Things have just been great recently." Garrett narrows his eyes for a beat. Skepticism written in the lines of his forehead. But I don't cave under his inspection. An unfamiliar scrutiny. "Can't I just be happy?" I add for good measure.

He leans back and relaxes in his chair, hands in prayer at his chin. Then he drops them to his side and smiles brightly. "Of course, man." He sits straighter and rolls his chair back. "Just wondering if you finally ditched Kelli."

Kelli.

My phone pings on the table and I flip it over to see a text notification. *Kelli Langston.* As if the queen of entitlement heard her name spoken. With a shake of my head, I roll my eyes.

Kelli: Have lunch with me.

My fingers dash over the keyboard, but before I hit send on *not today*, Kelli walks through the door as if meetings are above her. As if client confidentiality doesn't apply when she is in the room.

How the hell did she know I was in here?

"Hey, guys. Hope I'm not interrupting."

She plasters on her plastic smile while tucking a blonde lock behind her ear. We all know she gives two shits about interrupting people. Why? Kelli Langston is Stone Bay "royalty." The youngest in the Langston family. One of the Stone Bay seven.

Physically attractive, Kelli turns heads no matter where she goes. During the town's fall festival last year, she turned mine. Not that I hadn't seen Kelli in town prior, but it had been the first time she noticed me. The chemistry between us had been undeniable the first few months.

Then something flipped.

She went from sweet and endearing to overtly posses-sive. Every time my phone chimed with a notification—email, text, call, social media—she hounded me with ques-tions. Who it was. What they wanted. She wanted the passcode to my phone. To read through texts and emails. To monitor my calls.

Don't get me wrong, I like a woman that knows what she wants and goes for it. But her demands to invade my privacy as well as the clients who reached out to me, that is when I drew the line. Broke things off with her.

Or so I thought.

In my eyes, Kelli and I aren't a couple. I told her as much countless times. With each breakup, she waves it off with a laugh. Tells me I am ridiculous for thinking she would ever leave my side.

Doesn't help that I fan the flame—joining her for the occasional lunch or party at her parents' estate. No matter which way I spin it, Kelli Langston doesn't understand the word *no*. Nor does she comprehend people not caving to her wishes.

Just as I say, "We're in a meeting," Garrett says, "No bother. We were wrapping up."

Thanks. For nothing.

"Did you see my text?" Before I get a word in, she

continues, as if my answer is irrelevant. "Was thinking we'd hit the diner." She fans out her fingers and studies the blush polish. "I'll be at the car." She spins on her heel and walks out.

"Wow," Terrance states, eyes wide, brows at his hairline. "Did that just happen?"

Terrance and Garrett are all too familiar with Kelli and her *the world revolves around me* mentality. But it is rare for them to see it in action. Considering she was once my girlfriend, and the firm handles the Langston's investments, there is no escaping Kelli. Not anytime soon.

"Yep." The last letter pops on my lips. "Drives me insane." I look at the guys. "How many times do I break up with her before it sticks?" I drag my fingers through my hair. "Jesus. Hiring hit men isn't my thing, but if it works…"

Terrance joins my laughter. Garrett, not so much.

"She can't be *that* bad," Garrett offers.

I raise my brows in question. "Oh, no? You ever had a tick burrow itself into your skin? 'Cause that's pretty much what she's done. And I can't seem to dig her out."

Garrett shrugs as he gathers his belongings. "Whatever. Meeting's over. Enjoy your lunch." And then he disappears.

I look to Terrance. "Am I reading too much into it or did Dunn seem upset over what I said?"

Terrance closes his padfolio and rises from his seat. "Don't worry about him. Think he's having girl trouble."

From what Garrett shared, he has been dating Ann for

years. He never shared much about her with us, just that he loved her and planned to propose soon. Maybe he did and shit hit the fan. But he'd ask us for advice at that point. Right?

No telling. He will share more in his own time. Until then, I lend an ear and curb my own issues.

"Enjoy lunch," Terrance teases on his way out.

"Thanks," I deadpan. "Maybe I'll get lucky and come back without extra weight."

"Good luck," he says on a laugh.

I need all the luck I can get.

FIVE

SKYLAR

"WAS GOOD SEEING YOU," Oliver says, wrapping an arm around my shoulders and kissing my head. "You get good pics today?"

I melt into his side as I swipe through the pictures on my phone. One after another, I share the food and restaurant shots I'd taken for Poke the Yolk, a breakfast/brunch destination in Stone Bay. One of five food establishments owned by Calhoun-Kemp Industries—my employer.

As the company's social media marketing manager, I visit each location biweekly and take photos to post online. My job isn't just to entice the locals to stop by and spend their hard-earned money, but to also lure in the tourists. Make lattes, pancakes, club sandwiches, and steak dinners drool-worthy on screen. Which is easier said than done.

The kitchen staff is ready for me on each visit. Plating

the food as if it were entering a competition. Doesn't hurt that I get to sample the goods too.

"Yeah. Maxine made phenomenal strawberry-Nutella crepes today," I say, stopping on the image.

Oliver drops his arm and takes the phone, zooming in on the shot. "No one makes crepes like Max. Great shot." He hands me the phone and we inch apart.

Oliver Moss. Eleven months and one zodiac sign are all that separate us. When Mr. Calhoun hired him three years ago, I practically stalked him. Came to the restaurant every other day to eat, grab a coffee, or share small talk with the new busboy. I had been enamored with his short, dark curls and basil-green eyes.

The more I got to know Oliver, the more I realized we would never be more than friends. Not after I figured out he crushed on his best friend, Levi. At first, I had been devastated. Bummed I missed out on a good guy. Then, it dawned on me how lucky I was.

Oliver—Ollie—is one of my best friends. An unbreakable bond better than any romantic relationship. Well, better than any I'd had to date.

I pocket my phone and fetch my purse from beneath the counter. "On to RJ's I go."

"One day, you'll do your rounds when I have the day off. Let me be your assistant."

"Since when do I need an assistant?"

"Since you can't eat all the food yourself." He tilts his head and makes a face. "I'm more than happy to resolve the issue," he offers, patting his stomach.

Rolling my eyes, I walk past him, enter the kitchen, and head for the back door. "I'll see what I can do," I holler as I step outside. I don't miss his "Yes!" before the door closes.

My drive from Poke the Yolk to RJ's Diner & Dive passes in two songs. I park in the back and shoulder my purse before locking the car.

I smell Ray Jr.'s famous chili and cornbread-battered onion rings before setting foot inside. My mouth waters instantly. Of the five stops I make today, RJ's is my favorite. Hands down. I have eaten everything on the menu and still can't choose a favorite. All are my favorite.

I stow my purse in the office and stroll through the kitchen, stopping near the flattop. "Hey, RJ."

Gentle, umber-brown eyes crinkle at the corners before looking my way. "Hey, darlin'. Photo day already?"

"Yup." I eye the fried egg he slides on a plated cheese-burger with all the fixings. "Thought I'd take a handful of staff and restaurant pics before getting to the good stuff."

"You got it, darlin'. Tell Sandi when you want the first order."

The day before I do my rounds, I email the CKI establishments with a list of what foods I want to photograph. This keeps me from repeating images. 'Cause if I chose when I arrived, I'd pick the same food each go around.

"Will do. Thanks, RJ."

Before exiting the kitchen, I snap photos of RJ while he cooks and his son, Ray III, chopping at the prep station. In the dining room, I scan the interior for the perfect restaurant shots. I capture a few before getting some of the waitstaff. On my way to an open table near the windows, I tell Sandi I am set whenever the kitchen has food ready.

While I wait, I open the sent email to read over the list for RJ's. Once I get my shots in, the food goes to the back for staff to eat. All except one. The blueberry pie milkshake and chili cheese fries are mine today.

After reading over the list, I survey the booths and tables. The social media posts don't include patrons unless there is a big celebration (and we get their permission) or the image is cropped to remove faces. The food and employees remain the focus, but that doesn't stop me from searching for great shots.

I freeze when my eyes hit the back corner near the bathrooms. A great shot isn't what grabs my attention across the dining room. Nope, it's the blonde. Sitting with Lawrence. A woman known by the majority of the residents. Kelli *Bitchface* Langston.

Sandi deposits a bowl of chili with shredded cheddar and a tower of cornbread-battered onion rings on the table. "You alright, Sky?"

I take a deep breath to center myself, force a smile, and meet her eyes. "Yeah, I'm good. Just saw something unsavory."

"Don't you fret. You'll have that milkshake and fries in no time."

My smile turns genuine. "Thanks, Sandi. I'll be ready for the next one in a few."

"Take your time." She winks and walks off to check on a customer.

Sliding out of the booth, I position the food and snap a photo. I do this a few times, changing angles and layout. While I wait for the next dish to arrive, I open my text history with Lawrence, then look up to see Bitchface lay her hand on his. He doesn't seem keen but doesn't shirk away either. I grit my teeth and type a message.

Skylar: You hook up with people in diners too?

I hit send, then stare across the restaurant.

I may be young, I may be shy, but I am not naive. And I am damn sure not somebody's sidepiece. Not now. Not ever.

His phone chimes and he all but tears his hand away from her. It takes to the count of four before his eyes dart across the room and land on me. Panic widens his eyes as he scoots out of the booth, excuses himself, and walks my way. Kelli's jaw drops as she follows him with her eyes. When they land on me, her lip curls.

A couple years back, Kelli added me to her shit list. She had come into the main office of CKI, wanting to reserve Calhoun's Bistro for an evening. I denied her. Told her we don't close off the entire restaurant for parties, but offered the private room in the back. Needless to say, she was pissed and demanded to speak with my boss, Roger Kemp. Unfortunately for her, Mr. Kemp allowed me to make business decisions. I took down her information and said I'd forward the complaint to him. When I did, Mr. Kemp said to email her with the same answer, with his signature at the bottom. Since then, there has been an underlying anger between us. Thankfully, I don't see her in town much.

Shitty that the first time I see her in months, Lawrence is across from her.

"It's not what it looks like," he says as he slides in the booth.

"No?" I lace my fingers and set my hands on the table. "What is it then?"

He huffs, drops his eyes to the table, and shakes his head. "It's complicated."

"Uncomplicate it until I understand."

Lawrence brings the heels of his palms to his eyes, digging his nails into his scalp. Gone is the dark, edgy man from the pub. This Lawrence is frustrated and annoyed and fed up. The longer he sits in silence, the angrier I get. Sandi points to a Reuben with potato salad and a pickle. I hold up my hand for her to wait.

Dropping his hands, Lawrence straightens in his seat. He looks off to the side and shakes his head. Already, I hate where this is headed.

"Yes, we dated. I broke it off. More than once. But she hasn't gotten the memo."

How hard is it to break up with someone? *Things aren't working. Peace out.* Seems pretty straightforward.

"Well, until she does"—I gesture between the two of

us—"this can't happen. I don't need her drama or to be branded with a scarlet letter."

Although… the idea of tarnishing Kelli's image has me warm and fuzzy.

"*Fuck.*" He hangs his head.

And then an idea sparks. "Mmm. Soon, I hope."

How do I detach myself from Kelli?

Stupid. Fucking. Question.

Dating isn't like marriage. You don't get a certified document when it starts or ends. It just happens. But how does it work when one party refuses to let go? Do I stand in the middle of RJ's, the eyes of thirty plus townspeople on me, and confess my nonexistent relationship with Kelli Langston?

Embarrassed as she'd be, that won't push her away. She'd simply retaliate. Make a mockery of me.

Skylar sits motionless across the table, arms crossed and pushing up her breasts, lips shifting left to right. Her gaze holds mine, darkness rimming her jade irises. A hidden trick up her sleeve.

"Why so quiet?"

A conniving smile tugs at her lips. The look rests oddly

on her delicate features. Her eyes drift across the restaurant, then meet mine again. "Wasn't kidding when I said I don't need her drama. But..."

"But what?" My tone harsher than I intended.

"She believes you're in a relationship?" I nod. "But you don't?"

I really hate repeating myself. "Correct. Can't seem to shake her."

"What do you think *would* shake her?" Skylar straightens her spine and rests her forearms on the table, leaning forward. If I had the answer, Kelli would have been gone long ago. "A woman like her keeps up with appearances. Wants people to look up to her. Bow down to her."

Where is the reserved woman I met weeks ago? The one who sat at the bar, sipped her beer, and resisted dancing with her friend. Skylar and I haven't spent time together since that night, but we chat daily. I may not *know* her, but I never sensed this side of her. A darker side.

This side is fucking hot.

Never understood the adage *watch out for the quiet ones* until now.

I peer over my shoulder, spot the sneer on Kelli's lip before she replaces it with a fake smile. "All true," I say as I turn back to face her. "But it takes a lot to ruffle her feathers."

"There're a few things that may work." She cocks a brow.

"Should I worry? Your love for serial killers isn't taking over, is it?"

Her lips tip up at the corners. "You flatter me, but no need to worry. I have a better idea."

"Oh, yeah?"

She bites her lower lip and my cock pulses beneath my zipper. "Mmmhmm. I want you to go back to your table, give her whatever story you want about me, then invite her over for dinner."

I lean back, my knee grazing hers under the table, and tilt my head, confused. "You want me to invite her to my house?" She nods. "For dinner?"

"Yep. Except there won't be a dinner."

"There won't?" I ask, utterly fascinated with the devious angel opposite me.

For the most part, I live life on the straight and narrow. Punctual for work and gatherings. Kind to others. Always there to lend a hand. A basic regimen I follow in my personal life. The only disruption is when I placate Kelli. Join her for a social event. Act as her arm candy to keep her happy, all for the sake of my job.

But I need out.

Hopefully Skylar's idea doesn't involve getting shoved in the back of a police cruiser. At twenty-three, Skylar is more mature than most women my age—Kelli included. But her revenge plot may be more juvenile with less life experience. Fingers crossed it's not.

"Nope."

She inches forward and I mimic the action. Quickly, she outlines her idea and I listen to every detail. With the basic plan laid out, we decide to iron out the specifics after work.

Regardless if the plan works or not, tonight will be unforgettable. Because Skylar will be in my house. In my space. In my bed.

I palm my dick under the table and groan. "Fuck, I want to kiss you."

She licks her lips. "Plenty of time for that later. Now..." Scooting back, her leg grazing mine again, she waves over the server. "Get to work. I'll text you later."

After a quick adjustment, I exit the booth and walk back to Kelli. The closer I get, the more eager I am to get the ball rolling. This charade of hers has gone on too long.

"What'd *she* want?" Kelli asks with disgust bitter on her tongue.

"Calhoun-Kemp is catering an event for us. She's been trying to update me, but we keep missing each other." The lie rolls off my tongue easily. Not difficult when the person across from you is as artificial as they come.

"Well, prepare to be disappointed. She's trash."

My blood boils at her words, but I dampen the flame. Remind myself this will all be over soon. Tell myself Kelli won't be an issue much longer.

Not after tonight.

Finishing half of my club sandwich, I ask the server to box up the rest. I hand her my card for the check and she scurries back to the kitchen. She dashes back with the receipt and my leftovers before wishing us a good day.

I exit the booth and wait for Kelli to do the same. "Come to the house for dinner tonight."

"I, uh…" For the first time, Kelli hesitates. Maybe because I am initiating instead of her. Nonetheless, I find her reaction odd. For a woman who constantly inserts herself into my life, her hesitation gives me pause. "Yes, of course."

"You sure?" We walk toward the door, Kelli leading, and I wink at Skylar before stepping outside. "If you have other plans, we can do another night."

"Tonight works." She riffles through the gargantuan red purse on her elbow. "Thought I had something on the calendar with Daddy, but that's not tonight." Artificial laughter spills from her lips.

Is she hiding something? Color me intrigued. Part of me wants to dig up that dirt.

"Great. Seven?" She nods and presses unlock on the fob, slipping behind the wheel. "I'll leave the door unlocked."

Kelli gives me her well-practiced, fake-as-hell smile. "See you at seven."

I stand near the parking bump and watch Kelli exit the lot. When she disappears down the street, I face the diner window and nod at Skylar. Two spaces down, I get in the car and start it, but don't leave. Instead, I shoot Skylar a text.

Lawrence: She'll be there at 7
Skylar: When should I be there?
Lawrence: Any time after 5:30
Skylar: See you at 5:31 😄

Can't fucking wait.

SEVEN

SKYLAR

LAWRENCE HAS me park in the garage when I arrive. He leads me through the house and shows off the simple yet grand space. Two stories, four bedrooms, and more space than necessary for one person. When he guides me into his bedroom upstairs, I study the space intently.

A massive bed swallows most of the left wall; plush heather gray bedding offsets the charcoal-painted interior. I step farther into the room, scan over the black-lacquered wood furniture and minimal art above the bed and dresser. The room doesn't look lived in but smells of Lawrence. Of earth and musk with a hint of sweet.

I want his scent on my skin. The sooner, the better.

Lawrence steps up behind me, wraps his arms around my waist, and presses a kiss to my shoulder. "Leave your things up here." He sweeps my hair aside and kisses up the side of my neck. "I plan to bring you up here later."

"I may not leave," I tease.

He sucks my earlobe and adds teeth. "Who said I'd let you?"

Spinning in his arms, I crush my lips to his. Kiss him feverishly with tongue and teeth and hunger. Tug at the hem of his shirt, yank it up and break the kiss to toss it aside. Work the button and zipper of his jeans as he peels away my cotton tee. He reaches for my shorts as his jeans pool around his ankles. As I kick off my shorts, Lawrence takes a step back. He palms his cock; erection thick and pleading to escape his briefs. His eyes rake over me, cheeks reddening at the sight of my sheer bra and panties.

"I need to be inside you, little phoenix." He pinches the head of his cock. "Bare." The last word a growl, a *this is not up for debate* statement.

My skin heats at the idea of having nothing between us. "I'm on the pill. And clean."

He steps closer, reaches out, and clamps down on my fabric-covered nipple. I suck in a breath and reach for his cock. "I had a vasectomy years back." I freeze. Meet his swirling brown irises. "Story for another time. But I'm clean too."

As his hands snake around my bust to unclasp my bra, I push his briefs down and lick my lips as his cock springs free. When my bra joins his briefs on the floor, I drop to my knees and peek up at him.

His hand cradles my cheek. "What're you doing, little phoenix?" he groans out, cock twitching an inch from my lips.

"I want a little taste."

"I won't come down your throat. Not yet." I push out my bottom lip. "Later. If you're a good girl."

Drawing an *X* over my heart, I bat my lashes and say, "I'll be your good girl."

Fisting his cock, I lick up his shaft from root to tip before taking him in my mouth. A string of curses spills from his lips and I moan around his girth. His fingers comb through my tresses, curl into a fist, and hold me in place while he controls the pace.

"*Fuck*." He pumps harder, hits my gag reflex, and I reach around to bury my nails in his glutes. "I want to bruise these pretty lips." *Moan*. "Choke you with my cum." *Moan*. "Fuck every hole until your legs buckle." Eyes on him, I reach between my legs, dip my hand in my thong, and toy with my clit. He freezes, eyes my hand, and clucks his tongue. "That's for me."

He frees himself from my lips and hoists me upright. Before I voice my disappointment, he shoves my panties down, picks me up and tosses me on the bed, and dives between my thighs.

"Oh, God," I moan out, fisting his hair.

"Welcome to the Holy Land, little phoenix."

It isn't long before I writhe beneath his tongue and reach the pearly gates. Too soon, he scoots off the mattress and offers his hand. I slip my hand in his, rise off the bed, and follow him downstairs; our clothes forgotten.

We enter the kitchen, a marble-top island separating the space from the living room, and Lawrence picks me up and sets me on the counter near the sink. I take in the stainless steel appliances, black marble counters, and pristine white cabinets. A coffee maker, fruit basket, and cookbook stand are all that sit on the counters. Aside from a lonely basil plant on the windowsill.

"I planned to cook you dinner," he says, then checks the time on the oven. "But there isn't time." He parts my legs and steps between them. "Want a snack? Some cheese and fruit?"

"Sure."

He plants a kiss on the tip of my nose, then goes to the fridge. Rummaging through, he takes out a block of cheese, grapes, and berries, then retrieves a knife from a drawer. One by one, he cuts off small chunks of cheese and feeds them to me with a bite of fruit between.

"After," he holds a blueberry to my lips, "I'm feeding you."

"You are feeding me." I snatch the berry from his fingers.

"No." He scoots me closer to the ledge, wedges himself between my legs, leans in and takes my nipple in his mouth. "I want to make you a meal." He latches on to the opposite breast and sucks. "And I want to feed it to you." His tongue trails down my midline and I gasp. "Then eat from you." Heat pools between my legs as he circles my clit. "Possess you."

And then his mouth is gone. Goose bumps flare as cool air bites my skin. I open my mouth to protest as he stands, but before the words form on my lips, he is there. The tip of his cock at my entrance. Thick and hot. Pulsing and ready. He licks from my chin to my nose.

"Let me possess you, little phoenix." His tip glides up and down my slit. Teasing. Torturing. "Let me take care of you."

He leans in, going for a kiss, but I tilt my head and expose my neck. Wet heat sparks beneath my ear and sends my eyes rolling back. I rake my nails down his spine until I reach his ass. Grab hold and pull him to me as I rock forward.

My moan and his hiss collide in the middle. His hands snake around my waist and drag me forward, into him, onto him. Rough and deep and so fucking glorious.

Another shift has me barely on the counter. His tongue on my lips, my jaw, my ear. "Hold on to me."

I do as he says. Claw my way up the sides of his spine. Drape my arms over his shoulders. Lock my ankles above his ass. And then he moves. Rocks his hips forward. Fills me fully. Stretches me deliciously. One of his arms locks around my hips while the other glides up my spine, his hand fisting the back of my neck. Pinning me in place while he pistons in and out.

My whimpers blend with his throaty moans. The scent of sex and the echo of ball slapping fill the room. Primal and raw and unrestrained.

Then I open my eyes. Catch an obstructed view of the room. See *her*. See the rage and disgust and embarrassment bloom on her face.

All it does is provoke me further. Goad me to rub more salt in her proverbial wound.

My mouth turns up at the corners. A mischievous smile on my lips before I fist Lawrence's hair, yank his head to the side, lick the line of his jaw and stop at his ear. "Possess me, Law. Make me yours."

He growls loud enough for her to hear. Inches his fingers into my locks, fists the curls, and yanks my head back. Hard. My breasts to the ceiling as he licks down my neck, stopping at the fleshy skin above my collarbone and sinking his teeth in. I cry out—a heady mix of pleasure and pain.

"Who owns you, little phoenix?" he asks, hips rocking more vigorously.

"You do," I stammer.

He yanks my hair again; a sharp sting at the roots. "Say the fucking words, little phoenix."

A guttural moan rips from my throat. "You own me, Law."

"Fucking right I do."

Teeth bite my shoulder; sharp and vicious. My body a swarm of sensation. I sink my nails into his skin. Squeeze my legs around his frame. Then I plummet headfirst into euphoria seconds before Law pulls out and marks his territory. Paints my skin, my breasts, my throat, my face with his ownership.

I lick my lips. Taste his seed on my tongue. Then smile wickedly as Kelli turns on her heel and storms for the door.

Bye, bitch.

If Lawrence fucking me on the counter doesn't send a clear message, I will figure out more delicious and devious ways to get it through her head. Kelli Langston thinks Lawrence is hers, but she has never been more wrong. Because this man... he is all *mine*.

EIGHT

LAWRENCE

SOMETHING ISN'T ADDING UP.

I review the Barron's portfolio—for the third time—before our meeting at eleven. For the life of me, I can't figure out how they are missing more than ten thousand since pulling up the accounts yesterday. If they had funds in aggressive, high-risk stocks, I would be less concerned. But Elouise and Clarence Barron have their money secured in low-to-no risk investments. Funds in 529 Plans for grandchildren and great-grandchildren. Trust funds set up for all the Barron heirs.

Comparing the printout from yesterday, I see the overall loss on the bottom line, but can't pin down which account within the portfolio it came from or where the money went to. Being a numbers guy, needing everything to add up to the penny, this pisses me off. Clients trust me and I will not be made to look a fool.

A soft knock taps against the doorframe and I peer up

from the data to see Garrett. He leans against the jam and crosses his ankles, cool as a cucumber while my heart balls up its fists and violently beats my rib cage.

"Ready for your meeting?"

No. Yes. No.

Either way, I have no choice in the matter. "Yep." I shuffle the papers on my desk and sit taller, hoping the change in posture will boost my confidence. "Gathering the documents now."

"Hmm." Out of the corner of my eye, Garrett straightens and studies me from the doorway. Something about his stare throws me off today. Sweat beads at my temples as I tidy the portfolio printout. "Sure you'll do fine."

Unease swells beneath my diaphragm, an unfamiliar sensation—at work and in my personal life. And I don't like it. Not one bit.

As if sensing my discomfort, Garrett steps back, mutters his farewell, and walks off to his office. Without his eyes on me, I feel less under the micro-scope. The unease lifts some, but not enough that the panic fades.

Get through this meeting. Then, sort out where the money went.

Fuck.

The office phone buzzes on my desk and I pick up the receiver. "Howell."

"Mr. Howell, Mr. and Mrs. Barron are here for your eleven o'clock."

I close my eyes and inhale as deeply and quietly as possible. "Thanks, Meaghan. I'll be up in a minute."

Parking the receiver back in the cradle, I take a second deep breath, hold it until my lungs scream, and release my thoughts from a moment ago.

Get through this meeting.

Who knows? Maybe there is a glitch with the software. A technology malfunction. It has to be that. Right? What other viable explanation is there?

By the end of the meeting, my armpits are drenched. I pray the unending sweat pools haven't leached into my dress shirt and my deodorant hasn't failed me. If so, Mr. and Mrs. Barron don't point it out.

We rise from our seats and shake hands before I guide them out front. Soon as they exit the building, I breathe easier. Although the problem isn't resolved, I no longer have them lingering while I search for answers. Thank whoever the hell watches over me that they didn't question their balances either.

The door click is ten times louder as I reenter my office and shut the door. The chair behind the sturdy mahogany desk complains as I sit. My head drops in my hands as the heels of my palms mash into my eyes.

How the hell will I fix this?

With no other in-office appointments today, I have

time to scour data for answers. Dig line by line until I get answers. The planned outbound calls can wait.

Wiggling the mouse, I wake up the computer and enter my credentials. As the Barron account loads on the screen, my phone buzzes in my pocket. I yank the device out to see a text notification from Skylar.

Skylar: Lunch?
Lawrence: Want to, but I need to work. Project.
Skylar: How about I deliver something? You need sustenance 😋
Lawrence: You're amazing. Thank you.
Skylar: Requests?
Lawrence: Whatever you get is fine.
Skylar: See you soon.

A foreign weight lifts from my shoulders. Knowing I have uninterrupted time to research the problem until the office closes. If necessary, I will spend all day locked in here, so long as I locate the issue.

Knee-deep in numbers, I startle when the desk phone buzzes. I tap the intercom button. "Howell."

"Mr. Howell, a Ms. York is at the front with a food delivery."

"Send her back, Meaghan. Thank you."

The office quiets when I disconnect and go back to my investigation. Over the last hour, I have found jack shit. My hands more than empty. Desolate. To say it irks me would be a fucking understatement.

Money doesn't just disappear overnight.

A light tap on the door draws my attention before it swings open. Meaghan gives me a quick smile before narrowing her eyes on Skylar. If I'd blinked, I would have missed it. She gestures for Skylar to enter, gives me one last tight smile, then closes the door.

Weird.

My stomach groans the second I smell the burger and fries. I close my laptop and push it aside as Skylar takes a seat across from me at the desk. I lean forward and she mirrors the action, our lips meeting in the middle.

"Thank you for lunch. I'd have skipped it otherwise."

"Everything okay?"

Since that night at the pub a month ago, Skylar and I have gotten close. Closer than any previous relationship. Daily texts or calls kept us connected the first two weeks. Seeing each other at her house or mine every day since the night in my kitchen. In that time, I have learned so much about my addictive siren with fiery locks.

Yes, the sex is mind blowing and intoxicating and endless. But I also enjoy her company. Enjoy the conversations and cuddles on the couch while watching her beloved documentaries. Her wrapped in my arms as often as humanly possible.

Most women Skylar's age are go, go, go. Out at bars or with friends or hooking up. Living the party life—wild and carefree. I am guilty of such things at her age. Not to say she hasn't done those things, but not many twenty-three-year-olds want to sit at home in pajamas with their boyfriend.

Boyfriend. Yep, we defined us.

After the Kelli incident at my place—such a shame I missed the look on her face while I pounded Skylar on the kitchen counter—I haven't heard a peep from her. *Thank fuck.*

The next morning, in my bed, I told Skylar I wasn't joking when I said I owned her. Yes, she is her own woman. Free to live her life. But she is mine, and I needed to be sure she understood what that entails. Seconds after I'd held her chin in my grip and she said, "I understand," she'd slipped beneath the sheet and shown me exactly how well she understood.

Fuck, I love her mouth.

"Yeah. No." I take a deep breath and shake my head. "I don't know."

She unwraps a burger and sets it in front of me, unwraps her own, then dumps the fries between us. We eat in silence a moment—me contemplative and her watching me with concern.

"Anything I can help with?"

I swallow down the bite. "I wish. Something isn't right with one of my clients and I'm not sure what to do."

"Are they sick?"

"No. Nothing like that." In my line of work, there isn't much I can divulge—confidentiality and whatnot—but I can skirt around numbers, not specific dollar amounts, but generic figures. "Earlier, I reviewed an account and noticed a discrepancy. Had I not looked at the account yesterday, I might not have noticed today."

Skylar retrieves a Dr Pepper from her purse and pops the can open, taking a sip and offering me a drink. I sip the sweet carbonated beverage and mull over the blank page of answers in my head.

Her eyes lock on mine and widen. "Do you think someone's stealing from accounts?" she whisper-asks.

I wave off the idea. "Probably just a computer glitch somewhere. One I need to fix ASAP."

But as her words sink in further, the unease from earlier returns. The notion that one of my trusted coworkers stole money from a client seems preposterous. Not that I dismiss the prospect, but I need to cross off every other possibility first.

We finish our burgers and fries in relative silence. I make a mental checklist of what I need to check and who I need to call. Answers may not show up today, but I won't give up until I unearth them.

Skylar circles around my desk and I swivel to face her. "Thank you for lunch."

Her hands come to my tie and she straightens the knot at my throat. "Glad to help." She bends and kisses me, sweeter than usual. "Your place or mine tonight? I'll cook."

I should take tonight to myself. Lock myself in my home office and spend every waking minute scouring the Barron investments for discrepancies. Sift through spreadsheets with a fine-tooth comb. I should. But staring at endless lines of numbers on a computer screen for twelve hours straight fucks with your head. Before you know it, none of it makes sense.

My hands settle on her hips as I lift my lips to meet hers again. "Mine. I'll let you know when I head out."

Another kiss, then she steps around the desk, shoulders her purse, and walks to the door. "Later, Mr. Howell." She waves her fingers at me as she twists the knob and exits the office.

My dick twitches as she says Mr. Howell and I bite my bottom lip. Now is not the time or place. I have more pressing issues to deal with. Like how ten grand disappeared and where the hell it went.

I flip open the laptop and dive back in, determined to get results. If I don't make headway, IT is my next call. The sooner I get answers, the better.

A glitch. It has to be a glitch. I refuse to believe otherwise.

NINE

SKYLAR

THE HOUSE GOES dark as I plate the steaks.

"Shit," I bite out as I stumble back to the stove with a hot pan in my hand.

Light shines from the living room as Lawrence steps into the kitchen with his phone flashlight on. "You okay?"

I shift the pan to the left, setting it on the burner, then bring my pinkie to my mouth. My skin hit the metal grate a split second, but it was long enough to sting the skin.

"Yeah. Just bumped the stove a second."

Lawrence tugs at my hand and examines the pink angry mark on my finger before kissing it. "Run it under water. I'll get the first aid kit in a minute." He guides me to the sink as if walking the few steps alone will injure me further. "Where's your phone?" he asks once the water cools my skin.

"On the counter." I jerk my chin toward the breakfast bar.

Fetching my phone, Lawrence taps on the flashlight and sets the phone beside me on the counter. He kisses my lips, then steps back.

"Be right back. Checking to see if the neighborhood is out too. Then I'll grab the kit."

"'Kay."

He wanders off and I dry my hand on a dish towel. The burn didn't break the skin, but it will sting a few days. I finish plating the rest of dinner—at least it finished cooking—and set the plates on the bar. Lawrence comes back to the kitchen, a scowl firmly planted on his face, a small box in his hand.

"We're the only one without power. Checked the breakers and everything's fine." He waves his phone. "Reported the outage, so hopefully it'll come back on soon."

I pat the barstool to my right. "While we wait, let's eat."

Before either of us takes a bite, Lawrence gently rubs a dab of ointment on the wound, secures it with a bandage, then kisses the minor injury. This tender side of Lawrence... I really like it when he gets rough, but damn, I like his caretaker side too.

The steak, potatoes, and honey carrots disappear from our plates as we talk about the rest of our days. Lawrence is no closer to an answer with his client's account. His frustration is evident in each word and hand flail. Sure, I deal with spreadsheets and clients for CKI, but mine are more about marketing stats and which restaurant needs more promoting. When it comes to the CKI's finances, I throw my hands up and step back.

When our plates clear, I take them to the sink. As I turn the faucet on to wash them, a knock sounds at the front door. Lawrence walks around the bar, presses his lips to my forehead, then heads for the door.

"Probably the power company. Be right back."

I scrub up the dishes as mumbled conversation drifts from the front door. I finish the last of the utensils when Lawrence walks back in, jaw clenched and lips in a straight line. That can't be good.

"Is it okay if we stay at your place tonight?" he asks, irritation evident in his voice.

Setting the fork in the rack, I spin to face him. "Yeah. Sure. What'd they say?" I point toward the front door.

Unhumorous laughter floats in the room, the sound churning the dinner in my belly.

"Someone cut the line."

My brows pinch together. "What?" I ask, confused.

Lawrence tips his head back and stares at the ceiling. He takes a deep breath. Then another. And another, before leveling me with his gaze. "Someone. Cut. The. Power." He shakes his head, not believing it himself. "Who can do such a thing? How? What the hell is going on?" he whispers, more to himself.

I step into him, wrap my arms around his waist, and kiss the base of his throat. "I don't know, Law." Leaning back, I study the shadowed lines of his profile. "But we'll figure it out. C'mon." I take his hand and lace our fingers. "Let's get what we need and go."

With a nod, he leads us back to his room, where he stuffs an overnight bag. He locks up the house and we drive our cars to my place. After minor conversation with Kirsten and Delilah, we head to bed, exhausted from the day. We hit the sheets and spoon, foregoing sex. And as Lawrence's hold around my waist relaxes, his breath low and rhythmic at my ear, I stare at the wall, wondering who the hell is fucking with him. It may only be a couple dots, but I will connect them.

The first person on my shit list? Kelli Langston. Because I took what she thought was hers with a fucking smile on my face.

TEN

LAWRENCE

AFTER A SHITTY WEEK and zero answers on why the Barron account is short and a hefty bill to fix a power line I didn't tamper with, a weekend with my girl is in order. Starting tonight with dinner at Calhoun's Bistro.

Yes, her employer owns the restaurant. No doubt she has eaten almost everything on the menu. But dinner with me at Calhoun's is different. My guess is she hasn't sat opposite a man, eyes locked, lit candle in her periphery, and shared a decadent, intimate meal in public. I better be the first. And last.

After a dab of cologne at my neck and wrists, I adjust the collar of my black button-down and comb my fingers through my hair. I step back from the bathroom vanity and give one final glance in the mirror.

When was the last time I wanted to impress a woman? I jog my memory. Search weeks and months. Recall the last time I purposely dressed to arouse the opposite sex. It has been far too long.

Before Skylar, Kelli had been the last woman I flashed a smile and begged for undivided attention. That was eight months ago at the Stone Bay Financial annual client appreciation banquet held each November. That was before I knew the real Kelli Langston. The woman who smiled for the crowd, flaunted her inheritance like a weapon, and didn't take no for an answer.

Had I known last fall how narcissistic Kelli is, that she would be more difficult to shake than a venereal disease, I would have passed on her dinner invitation. I would have said no from the start.

And damn, I have tried to shake her since late January without success.

All along, Skylar was the answer. The quiet woman who knows what she wants and isn't afraid to fight with fire. Little phoenix.

I pocket my wallet and keys, then send her a quick text.

Lawrence: Leaving now.
Skylar: Perfect timing. Almost ready.

The few miles between our houses vanish in no time. I park on the street and walk to the door. Before my knuckles rap the wood, the front door opens and her roommate, Kirsten, stands opposite me.

"Hey, Law." She tosses me a wave. "Come in. She'll be out in a sec."

My shoes clap the tiled foyer as Skylar enters from the hall. My feet glue to the floor as my eyes rake down her body. Take in the sight of her.

I swallow the lump in my throat and shift in place to adjust the bulge behind my zipper.

Skylar and I see each other every day. For dinner and the occasional lunch. For lazy weekends or hot nights between the sheets. The more time we share, the more addicted I become to my little phoenix. Right now, though... I may cancel dinner, take her home, and dine on her instead.

"Wow," I mutter as she steps into my space.

The forest-green dress hangs from thin straps at her shoulders. Silky fabric loose on her petite frame. A slit down her sternum exposes the medial swell of her breasts. The skirt swishes with the sway of her hips. A thin silver chain looped at the base of her throat and trailing between her cleavage.

My favorite smile plumps her cheeks as she flattens her palms on my pecs. "Right back atcha."

"We should go," I choke out. "Before I change our plans."

Her brow cocks, her smile morphing as devious thoughts enter her mind. "If you say so."

I wave over her shoulder to Kirsten, then guide Skylar to the car. The drive is filled with talk of our day and upcoming events.

With summer in full swing, the town is ready to entertain the residents and tourists alike. The town goes all out each year for Fourth of July, and this year will be no different. Concerts, food, kid-friendly events, and fireworks. CKI sets up food tents and donates to the fireworks display. Most businesses in Stone Bay contribute in some way and each year is better than the previous.

The valet hands over the ticket as Skylar and I exit the car. Her arm hooks with mine and we walk to the open door of Calhoun's Bistro. A young woman behind the podium stands taller and straightens her tie as we approach and she eyes Skylar.

What level of authority does Skylar hold at CKI?

"Hey Candace," Skylar greets the young woman.

"Ms. York."

More power than previously suspected. Which adds a new layer of fire to my little phoenix. A layer I am eager to peel off.

The hostess shifts her attention my way and gives a practiced smile. "Welcome to Calhoun's Bistro."

"Reservation for Howell."

The woman scans the computer screen, then meets our stares. "Follow me, Mr. Howell."

Seated at a table, the hostess hands us menus and rattles off the chef specials tonight. I don't hear a word as I ogle Skylar in the candlelight across the small, cloth-covered table. Skylar's foot crawls up my leg under the table and I stop breathing. It isn't the casual nature of her open display that has my lungs frozen. More that I didn't expect her toes to trail up my thigh as the hostess mentions bison tenderloin.

The hostess finishes her spiel, walks off, and I exhale.

I fist Skylar's foot beneath the table, lock onto her jade-green irises—a hint darker with her choice of attire tonight—and lean forward. "Be a good girl, little phoenix."

Her lips kick up in a half smile. "What if I'm not?"

I lick my lips as my thumb digs into the arch of her foot. "Then you may not get dessert."

She studies me a beat, gauging the truth in my words. Would I deprive her when we returned home? No. Fun as it might be to tease the hell out of Skylar, I would be depriving myself in the process. Lucky for me, she doesn't know how far I am willing to go. How long I can hold out. And I need to keep Skylar on her toes.

"Fine," she huffs out, gingerly removing her foot from my lap.

Tonight is like no other evening we have shared. With our hormones stowed, we order dinner and settle into deeper conversation. We sip wine and learn more about our pasts, family, and hobbies.

Aside from her obsession with crime documentaries, Skylar loves the outdoors. Hiking. Camping. Swimming when the weather allows. If it's in the thick of nature, she loves it. Her top bucket list item is to visit all the national parks. To date, she has visited three. As she describes the first, I formulate a plan to take her to the remaining sixty.

I share a glimpse of my past with her. Talk about my

parents—both retired—and brother, Alton. Three years younger, Alton has always been my best friend. We don't see each other often since work took him across the country, but we talk regularly and get together when schedules permit. After a brief glance around the dining room, I explain to her why I got a vasectomy.

Surprised she hadn't brought up the subject sooner, I tell her about the woman I met in college. How she swore up and down she was on the pill, clean, and wanted me bare. I put too much trust in her. Two months later, she was at my doorstep with a pregnancy test. Needless to say, I lost my shit. Fought her for a paternity test. And then, miraculously, on the day of my appointment, she was no longer pregnant.

I am not completely averse to children, but that incident changed my outlook—on dating and family—for years. When I had the money, I made sure no one could trap me the way she tried. I wanted to choose when such life-altering decisions affected me.

We order dessert and I excuse myself to use the restroom. Less than three minutes pass before I return to a closed-off Skylar. She may not be the most outgoing woman, but I have never seen her cower.

"What's the matter?" I ask, dropping to my chair and scooting closer.

She shakes her head. "Nothing. It's fine," she mumbles, fidgeting with the napkin on her lap.

"Skylar." I inch forward and reach for her knee under

the table. "Look at me." On a deep exhale, she meets my stare. "What's wrong?"

Her shoulders slump, and her eyes frown at the corners. "Oh, you know. Just the fine people of Stone Bay talking shit in not-so-whispered tones."

My brows pinch together. "Someone was nasty to you when I stepped away?"

"Not to my face, but the comment was directed toward our table. And meant for me to hear."

"Who?" I growl.

She reaches across the table and takes my hand. "Law, no. I appreciate you wanting to defend me, I do, but please don't stoop to their level." Her grip tightens on my hand. "Let's finish our beautiful evening. You can make it all better once we leave."

A lascivious grin dons her creamy, freckled face, and my decision is instant. The server delivers dessert and I ask her for the check. We devour the sweet confection before the bill is settled, then rush out the exit just as quickly.

Halfway between the restaurant and home, I turn toward the bay and park in an unlit lot.

"What are you—"

Unbuckling my seat belt, I shove the seat back, unbutton and unzip my trousers, and pull out my cock. Skylar's eyes linger on my lap as her tongue darts out to lick her lips. She unbuckles her own belt, twists in her seat, kicks off her heels, and hikes up the skirt of her dress.

"Play with my cock, little phoenix."

She doesn't do as I ask. Instead, she peels off the straps of her dress. Exposes her perky, petite breasts. Pinches her nipples until they form stiff peaks. I watch her with rapt attention. Dick twitching beneath my palm as I deliver slow strokes. Then, her hand dips between her thighs. Her bottom lip caught between her teeth. She leans back on the door, props one leg on the center console and the other on the dash.

This is when I discover she is bare beneath the dress. And fuck, my dick turns to marble.

"What if I play with you like this first?" she purrs.

Her fingers stroke up her slick folds, circle her clit, then stroke down before disappearing inside her.

"Jesus fuck, little phoenix."

I stroke myself without pressure, reach across and toy with her nipple, and listen to the sound of Skylar's arousal as she finger fucks herself. It isn't long before her legs tremble and her skin turns a luscious shade of red.

Before she comes completely down from her high, I drag her over the center console, frame my lap with her legs, and push inside her. I piston in and out of her. Fist her hips in a bruising grip and rock them up and down my cock. Then we both go over the edge.

I sit straighter and take her mouth with mine. "Couldn't wait. And I'm not sorry."

She rocks her hips, and I groan. "I'll never complain that you want me." She kisses the tip of my nose and moves back to her seat. "Now"—she buckles her belt and holds my gaze—"take me home and own me."

"Anything for you, little phoenix."

ELEVEN
SKYLAR

THE WHISPERS around town have become more than noticeable. Words like *tramp* and *hussy* and *slut* easily rolling off the lips of women as I pass. Hearing the slander since our dinner at Calhoun's—when an older woman brazenly called Lawrence a *cradle robber* after he passed her table on the way to the bathroom—only adds fuel to the fire. He didn't hear her, but she made certain I did.

Normally, such behavior wouldn't eat at my insides. When people were nasty, I usually let it roll off my shoulders and went about my day. Which is what I should do now. For whatever reason, I can't seem to let this go as easily. Something about the angry swarm of upper-class women coming at me with their venomous barbs hits different. Like a high school gossip mill on crack.

If I don't get clarity soon, I will crack.

Although Lawrence comforts me in countless ways, I

need words of wisdom and hugs from a friend. Which is why I am spending my lunch break at Page by Paige, the local bookstore where my roommate and bestie, Delilah, works.

Soon as I step through the entrance, I stop and inhale. What is it about bookstores that soothe the soul? The smell of new and well-loved pages. Ink imprinted on paper. Books and bookstores have been one of my happy places since early youth when Grandma Jean gifted me my first book. It has been downhill since.

I weave through the aisles and head for the section Delilah spends half her day in—romance. As I round the corner, laughter creeps up my throat. On a stool, Delilah has her eyes glued to the pages of the newest book in her most beloved series.

"Working hard?"

She startles, drops the book, and slaps a hand to her chest. "Damnit, Sky. You made me lose my page."

Now I let laughter spill free. "Must be nice to only worry about losing your page."

Rising from the stool, she picks up the book and shuffles through the pages. "At least I remember which chapter I was on." She slips a bookmark from her store apron and tucks it between the pages before stashing the book behind others on the shelf. "Here shopping?"

My shoulders cave. "I wish." I scan the immediate area and breathe easier when I spot no one. "Actually was hoping you could lend an ear."

"Yeah, sure." She spins around and starts down the aisle. "Let's go in the back."

We wind through romance and local indies before reaching a door marked *Employees Only*. She types a code in the door keypad and pushes inside. The break room looks like most others—table, chairs, time clock with punch cards in a holder, fridge, cabinets, and lockers for personal belongings. A unisex bathroom off to the left, no doubt cleaner than the public option.

Delilah fetches her metal, bento-style lunch box and water bottle from the fridge, parks herself at the table, and gestures for me to do the same. She opens the divided container, plucks a carrot stick and chomps away.

"So, what's up?"

Why didn't I think to grab food before stopping by? A sandwich from the deli across the street. Maybe a salad from the diner. Hell, even a side of fries would stifle my hunger pangs until I left.

As if reading my mind, Delilah scoots her lunch between us. A silent *eat whatever you want*.

"Thanks," I say, popping a grape in my mouth. "I'll restock some of your lunch foods next time I go shopping."

"Not necessary." She reaches for a boiled egg. "On to what matters."

Delilah is a great friend. The best. Had I known *who* she was before our friendship in high school, we would probably live different lives today. Considering her family is one of the seven, I would have avoided her from the start. Kept a distance. The Stone Bay elite didn't associate with people like me—lower to middle-class citizens.

But Delilah is different. Less pretentious. More open and loving. And I thank my lucky stars her last name didn't keep me from obtaining a best friend.

"I seem to have landed on the gossip radar."

Leaning in, she plants an elbow on the table and rests her chin in her palm. "Tell me more."

I roll my eyes. "Nothing has been said directly to me, but the whispers every time I pass someone on the street or in a store…" I shrug. "It's annoying as hell. They're trash-talking me like I'm the town whore."

Delilah sits back and laughs. Glad she finds the situation humorous. I sure as hell don't.

"Sorry." A hand covers her mouth. "It's just… you knew pissing off Kelli was like walking into the devil's lair without a plan. Right?"

Kelli hadn't consumed much of my time in the past. Yes, she got under my skin. As she did with countless others. But I never let her take up real estate in my mind. One—it would accomplish nothing. Two—who wants that woman in their head twenty-four seven? Not me.

"You think she started this? The whispers and nasty looks."

"Wouldn't be a shock. You didn't just step on her turf. You embarrassed her."

I point a carrot stick at Delilah. "How did I embarrass her? No one but her saw me and Law. He'd been trying to ditch her for months. I helped. Period."

Delilah nods and grabs a handful of berries. "True. But now you and Law are public. Out doing things together. Kelli may have started the rumor mill. She may be perpetuating the trash talk, but you out in the open with Law is gasoline on an already lit fire."

I toss down the carrot. "This is fucking ridiculous. So, what? I can't be out in public with my boyfriend?"

On a long exhale, Delilah reaches across the table and takes my hand. "Of course you can. But until she quits her childish games, your life will probably be like this. It sucks, but the snobs of this town coddle her. They hear her bullshit stories, her woe-is-me blather, and they automatically peg the other person the villain."

Delilah's family may be one of the Stone Bay originals, but at least they don't have a holier than thou mentality. After we had been friends a few months, Delilah told me the Fox way of thinking started to change with her grandparents. They attended exclusive events less often. Associated themselves with more townsfolk than elite. Then passed that way of life down the line to their children and so on. Yes, they still owned a chunk of Stone Bay. Yes, they still had more money than I would in two lifetimes. But they now used their assets and status for good.

Every day I had my friend, I silently thanked her grandparents.

"When does it stop, DeeDee? When do I get to live like everyone else?"

Her lips purse as she shrugs. "She needs a new plaything or someone else to torture." She cracks open her water, takes a sip, then offers me a drink. "Or…"

Cool water rolls down my throat. "Or what? You can't just say *ooor* and leave me hanging."

"What if you found dirt on her?"

Dirt? On Kelli Langston?

Seems damn near impossible to find anything unsavory about one of the town's princesses. Plus, do I want to get into a showdown with her? Stoop to her level and fight dirty. Pick apart someone's life so I feel better about my own. The idea swirls like poison in my gut.

"I may not like what she's doing, I may not like *her*, but I'm not that cutthroat. Embarrassing her behind closed doors is not the same as making a public mockery. People will defend her much quicker than me and I'll be thrown to the wolves or shunned or who knows what."

After a quick squeeze, Delilah releases my hand. "That's why I love you. You have a great heart." She closes up her lunch and stows it in the fridge. "You don't need to slander her, but I still say you dig up what you can." I rise from the seat and follow her out. "She won't give up until you or Law find a way to make her stop. Sometimes, the threat of exposure is enough." Delilah grabs my shoulders and levels me with her gaze. "Dig. Deep."

Something about those last two words sits different. Like Delilah *knows* a secret, but can't share. So, I heed her advice.

"I will, DeeDee. Promise." Warm arms wrap around me and wash away some of the earlier pain. "Thank you."

She kisses my cheek, then releases me. "Now, go. Be productive and brilliant."

"Love you."

"Love you back."

TWELVE

LAWRENCE

"EVERYTHING OKAY?" Terrance asks as he steps into my office. His eyes home in on and study the IT guy I have had behind closed doors for hours.

"Fine. Just my computer acting up." The fib rolls off my tongue too easily.

Glen Princeton was a friend since early college. We never shared dorm space, but ran in similar circles and shared the same morals. I trust Glen and the feeling is mutual. Which is why I reached out to him after days of no answers on the Barron account.

Glen hacked tech with the best of them. And he did so legally. After hacking a multimillion dollar company years back, instead of prosecution, the company hired him. Paid him a tremendous salary to prevent future invasions.

So, when I needed to find the culprit behind my tech issue, once I had crossed every possibility off my list, I called Glen.

"Hope it gets fixed." Terrance stuffs his hands in his slacks and steps to my desk. "Want to grab a bite? I forgot lunch today." Terrance shifts his weight left to right and back again. His eyes refusing to meet mine.

What's up with him?

Terrance isn't one to be anxious. He may be the youngest in our office pod, but he always stands tall and speaks with confidence. Never dishes out bullshit to attain clients—one of his best traits. That said, seeing him fidget is new. Seeing him fidget has me concerned. Because Terrance doesn't fidget. Ever.

"Sounds good. Let me lock up the office. Meet you out front?"

Eyes zeroed in on my laptop, he nods. Without a word, he exits the office and walks down the hall.

Weird.

Terrance sips iced tea while we wait for lunch to be delivered to the table. His nervousness waned slightly, but not enough to keep his fingers from rolling the straw wrapper every other second.

Rosenberg's Delicatessen is slow at the moment, the lunch rush undoubtedly bombarding the place an hour earlier. But the place remains open all day for those wanting more than just a quick bite. Aside from sandwiches, the deli offers an array of sides, heat-and-eat meals, and select groceries.

"So," I say, unwrapping my own straw. "What's up with you?"

Setting his cup on the table, Terrance glances around the deli. His shoulders loosen when he sees the place still empty. He leans forward, covering half the table with his forearms. "Have you noticed anything off recently?"

"Off?"

Several things have been *off* in the last few weeks, but I don't know the motive behind his question. From the discrepancy on the Barron account to the power outage to the whispers, I have no clue what Terrance knows or where he stands. Hell, this could be a ploy. A way to get me to spill something he doesn't know. Not happening.

Terrance needs to show his cards before I show mine.

He looks left and right, then meets my waiting gaze. "The tech guy... have any of your accounts been tampered with?" My eyes narrow as I hold his stare. *Gonna have to give me more, Terrance.* "I had a meeting with Roger Emerson the other day. Beforehand, I reviewed his portfolio like I always do. The figures don't add up."

My eyes widen. Jaw drops.

What. The. Hell?

First, the Barron account. Now, the Emerson account. Has someone hacked the Stone Bay Financial database? Is someone skimming accounts? Seems the only logical explanation. How, though? Our firewall, from what I had been told, is impenetrable.

Once Glen has answers about the Barron account, I will ask him to research Terrance's problem next.

That said, I choose my next words wisely. Terrance has given me no reason to not trust him. Has never acted schemy. But what if he is the mastermind behind it all and this is him digging for details? Checking in to see if I noticed the change in the Barron account.

The twinge in my gut tells me to proceed with caution. To not open up and share.

"What do you mean they don't add up?"

He takes a deep breath, then sits back, palms flat on the table. I watch for any tells, any possibility of deception as he speaks. "So, we aren't required to check client accounts weekly or even monthly, but I do. I like to keep an eye out. Forewarn of possible loss before a stock nosedives."

"That's what makes you an awesome portfolio manager," I praise him.

"Thanks." A clipped smile dons his lips. "Since I do this, I know when changes hit. When I compared the recent figures to the last printout in their file, the numbers didn't add up. The overall balance of the portfolio was the same, but one of the investments is off."

"How much?"

A young man steps up to the table with two plates. "Pastrami on rye; side of potato salad." Terrance holds up a hand. The young man deposits the plate on the table. "Means the ham and turkey with macaroni salad is yours."

I nod. "Anything else, gentlemen?" We both shake our heads and he walks back to the counter.

Once alone again, Terrance spears a potato. "Twenty grand."

Had I taken a bite of lunch, I would have choked. "What the fuck," I whisper-growl.

"Been staring at the figures all day and can't make sense of it."

We both dig into our meals, quiet and contemplative, as we try to make sense of what is happening. Two accounts. Thirty thousand unaccounted for.

As of now, I have no answers. But I will get them. No matter what. Glen will study the code, line by line, until he reveals the culprit. His services may cost a pretty penny, but eliminating the criminal is worth the price. And if I know Glen, he won't back down until he unearths the truth.

"Is that why you have an outside techie looking at your computer?" Terrance asks, washing down his lunch with more tea. "Is one of your accounts off too?"

Say Terrance is full of shit. Say this is all a ruse to figure out if I am onto whatever heist is going down. What will he do if I say yes?

If Terrance is part of the scheme, will he urge Glen to dig deeper? Or will he get defensive and say the firm's tech department should handle the issue?

Either way, I need answers. And I need to navigate this with the utmost discretion. The less who know, the better.

Before long, I will figure out who to trust. And who to put behind bars.

"Yep," I say on a nod. "I trust him. And seeing as I don't know who's behind the problem, it's better to have a trustworthy, outside source sort it out."

"Couldn't agree more." He presses a napkin to his lips. "Mind if he checks my computer next?"

"No problem. When we get back, I'll ask. Long as he's not busy with work, he'll more than likely help."

Terrance's entire frame sags. "Thanks, man. Last thing we need is clients thinking we're embezzlers." He sips his tea. "Didn't spend years of my life and thousands of dollars on my education to be tossed in jail for false accusations."

Felony embezzlement is not something the financial realm takes lightly. Years in prison and thousands in fines. All depends on the theft. Not to mention, you will never be trusted with money again. Ever. That charge would haunt anyone for life.

"Agreed." I scoot back from the table, stash a tip beneath my cup, and rise to leave. "I'll talk to Glen. For now, though"—I hold his stare, never more serious—"let's keep this between us."

Terrance nods. "Thanks for lunch, man. I'll let you know if anything changes."

THIRTEEN

SKYLAR

THUMP. Thump. Thump.

I throw on my blinker and pull onto the shoulder. After checking the mirrors for traffic, I ease out of the car and walk to the passenger side. Where I discover the rear tire, flat.

"Damnit."

Squatting down, I inspect the tire and spot a nailhead in the sidewall. *Great.* Looks like I will be shopping at the dealership for a new tire soon.

As I lug the spare and jack from the back of the car, I think over my travels in the last few days. Had I driven through any construction areas? Not that I recall. Nails didn't always equate to work crews with hammers and drills. For all I know, I might have driven behind a work vehicle when a nail broke free. The likelihood seems far fetched, but what do I know?

Three videos on YouTube later, and the car hasn't

lifted more than an inch from the pavement. Not from a lack of trying. If only I had paid more attention to Dad when I got my first car. When he showed me, more than once, how to change the tire if I got a flat. Next time I see him, I will hang my head and ask for another demonstration.

Today is not that day. Today, I need help.

I open the insurance app on my phone and request roadside assistance. After I submit the request, the wait time flashes in red. *Estimated time of arrival: 45 minutes.* Spectacular. Not like I need to work or anything.

Back in the cab, I press the ignition and crank the air. The summer temperature is unseasonably warm for our part of Washington.

While I wait for assistance, I call work and update them on the delay. Considering it is after two, Roger tells me to take the rest of the day off and make up the time wherever possible. I really do love my job and boss.

Next, I call Lawrence. Not that I *need* to share every minute with him as it happens, but I would want to know if he had car trouble.

"Hey, little phoenix. What has my girl calling midday?"

The day is absolute shit, but Lawrence's voice alone makes it better. The low timber and the way he calls me little phoenix. Both alleviate my stress. Both make me melt. And damn... I wish he was here.

"Maybe I just needed to hear your voice," I purr over the line.

He chuckles. "Sweet as that is, I doubt that's why you called."

"No." I exhale. The stress of the situation waning a bit. "Got a flat tire and I'm waiting on roadside. Tried to change it myself, but that went nowhere fast."

"Need a ride? I'll come get you."

I shake my head, then remember he can't see me. "No. I'll be fine. Just hate sitting on the side of the road, waiting."

Papers shuffle in the background, followed by the creak of leather. "Okay, but let me know when roadside arrives."

"I will." I peek into the rearview and see nothing but trees and empty highway.

"Come to the house tonight and I'll make the day better with dinner, dessert, and cuddles on the couch."

I bite my lip, thinking of Lawrence spooned behind me while we eat Twizzlers and watch television. "Can we watch the show I added the other night?"

"If you're asking to watch *I am a Killer*, do you really think I'll object? No man in his right mind would deny a woman who asks this. Not unless *he* wants his story told in a documentary." He laughs, and I picture him shaking his head.

"Hey, mister. A lot can be learned by watching them. Don't you ever wonder what makes someone commit such heinous crimes?"

"No, little phoenix, I don't. I'm more curious why it fascinates you."

I shrug and bite my lip. "Not sure. Just always been intrigued. Kind of like sharks. Sure, they're deadly creatures, but there's so much about them we don't know or understand. Doesn't mean you'll catch me in the water with them."

Long as I can remember, I have leaned toward the darker, scarier, and understudied parts of life. Found myself engrossed in the human psyche. The workings of nature. Questioned what makes a person commit atrocities —not because I want to help them better themselves, but to understand their thought process in the moment.

Does that mean I have a few screws loose myself? Perhaps. But if I did, I would never act on impulse.

"Text when roadside arrives. I'll wrap up with work and see you after. Any dinner requests?"

After the day—hell, the week—I want comfort food. Carbs. Lots and lots of carbs. Delicious, low-nutrition calories to smother the whispers around town and patch the flat tire.

"Something with potatoes or pasta. Maybe both."

Lawrence chuckles. "Potatoes and pasta. Check." Silence sits between us for three breaths, followed by a heavy sigh from him. "See you in a bit."

The call disconnects after I say goodbye. Not long after, roadside appears and swaps out my tire with the spare. As suspected, the tire isn't patchable with the nail in the sidewall. The old man with kind eyes suggests two auto shops in the area that don't try to upsell or overcharge female clientele. I thank him for the suggestions, but leave out that my father works at the dealership where I bought the car. Dad will get me a new tire at wholesale cost. Still an expense, but not as steep.

Handing me a copy of the roadside invoice, he looks me square in the eye. "Don't take this the wrong way, Miss York." He pauses and looks off in the distance, as if searching for the right words. Once his gaze circles back, he points to the car. "Nails happen. I see it all the time. But where that one was and the type of nail..." The corners of his mouth turn down. "I'd bet money it wasn't an accident."

My brows scrunch together. "How do you mean?" Because I really want to know. I am no idiot, but never having dealt with nails in my tire and only hearing others' flat tire stories, this isn't my area of expertise.

"Nails in the sidewall tend to be closer to the tread. Maybe an inch off, at most. That nail is close to the rim and perfectly straight in the tire. On the tread, I wouldn't question it going in straight. On the sidewall, though... hate to say it, but someone did that on purpose. And on a tire, you wouldn't see easily."

Mind. Blown.

What the hell is going on?

Yes, I pissed off Kelli Langston. Yes, I took something —someone—away from her. Lawrence didn't belong to Kelli, though. Kelli thought—maybe still thinks —otherwise.

Would she really resort to hammering nails in tires? The job seems below her snobbish ways. The gossip and whispers and shaming? Those seem more her style—like a teenager trying to ruin someone's reputation. But a nail in the tire? I suppose it is possible. If anything, she would pay someone to do the dirty work.

And after this news, I have reached my wit's end with her. The sudden uptick in bullshit... it needs to end.

I hold out my hand to the kindly man. "Thank you..."

He takes my hand with a soft grip and shakes. "Buddy."

"Thank you, Buddy."

He returns to his work truck, cranks the engine, then honks as he drives off. I stare after the white truck with the word *Roadside* in bold letters until it disappears from view.

"Hate to say it, but someone did that on purpose."

His words flash in my head like a neon sign in the pub window.

I don't just need comfort food, I need an isolated place to let out my anger. A place to scream at the top of my lungs where people won't think I am being murdered. I need release. Because if one more thing goes haywire, I might lose it. Fully lose it.

And I am too pretty for jail.

FOURTEEN

LAWRENCE

By a chance miracle, I leave work thirty minutes early, which gives me time to stop for a few things at the store — namely, potatoes and pasta, but also a few other items for dinner.

The basket dangles at my side as I stroll from produce to the meat department. After the butcher wraps up two chicken breasts, I waltz through the store for the final ingredients. While I sift through the blocks of parmesan, an older woman passes me with a sneer on her lips.

"Should be ashamed," she mutters.

I drop the cheese in my basket and follow her. "Excuse me?"

She peers over her shoulder, eyes wide as a hand comes to her chest. "Why are you following me?"

Lengthening my stride, I step ahead and grab her cart to halt her. "If you don't want people following you, don't insult them."

A gasp leaves her lips. Faux shock plastered on her weathered face. I resist the urge to laugh at her pompous attitude. Barely.

"What you did to the Langston girl... you're disgusting. Despicable. *Cradle robber*."

First off, how does anyone know what I did or didn't do to Kelli? The only person to see me with Skylar was Kelli. To tell the townsfolk you walked in on your supposed boyfriend while he fucked another woman... I don't picture Kelli wanting to taint her image that way.

Maybe Kelli isn't who I think she is. Maybe she would blather to the town. Shed crocodile tears in front of the gossip mill as she discloses what she walked in on. Whether for sympathy or the spotlight or both.

Secondly... cradle robber? Seriously?

Yes, Skylar is young. But she is also an adult. A woman capable of making her own decisions. That night at the pub, she could have sent me away. Denied me the chance to know her.

But she didn't.

Age doesn't define us. Age was invented by humans. And now, the people of Stone Bay are using age as a weapon when they don't know the first thing about battle.

I step closer to the woman. Watch as she swallows and shifts her weight. "And what is it I did to Ms. Langston? Who, by the way, is a grown woman. Not a girl," I growl.

Another swallow, then she turns up her nose and takes a step back. "I saw the evidence." Her voice shaky as her grip on the cart tightens. "Disgusting. Now..." she says with a layer of venom. Her eyes drift down to my clenched hand on her cart. "If you'll excuse me."

Stunned, I release the cart. Hear the clap of her shoes as she walks off. But I remain rooted to the floor.

Evidence. What evidence?

This woman says she *saw* something. *Saw what?* Everything that happened was behind closed doors. Unless... *Fuck.* Is there a photo out in the open? An image of me and Skylar, exposed and vulnerable, for all to see. My blood runs cold at the possibility of a photo floating around town or beyond.

Shit, shit, shit.

This explains the whispers Skylar mentioned. The hushed slander aimed her way like sharpened blades. And when I get home, I plan to look into said evidence. See what needs to happen to dispose of it.

The cashier chats small talk with me as she swipes and bags my groceries. I slide my card into the reader as she bags the last item and enter my PIN. *Declined.*

What the fuck?

I damn well know my account has more than enough funds to cover the total. My face heats as I put a different card in the reader and fib about the card being expired. When the second card declines, I pull cash from my wallet and hand it over.

After I all but run to the car, I whip out my phone, open the bank app, and stare down at my accounts. My shoulders sag as I read the balance. Relief washes over me as I stare at the figures. My money's still there. *Thank god.*

"Why then?"

Why did both my cards decline if I had the funds? Because someone is toying with me. Because someone wants me publicly embarrassed.

Kelli.

But how?

Kelli has zero access to my accounts or personal information. Hell, she never made an effort to know me in our short time together. But Kelli has connections. Wouldn't surprise me if she called in a favor. If that holds true, she is in for a rude awakening. As is whoever helps her play this fucked-up game.

I press the ignition and connect my phone to Bluetooth. On the drive home, I phone the bank and speak with a representative I have worked with time and again. Confusion laces his voice as I hear him tap the keyboard.

"Not sure why your cards stopped working, Lawrence. It's like someone flipped a switch and turned them off."

"No way it's a glitch?" I ask, needing to be certain.

"Haven't had any other calls and I've never seen this happen. So, I'd say not a glitch. But I've got it fixed now."

"Thanks for your help, Will."

"No problem. Call if it happens again."

Better not happen again. "Will do."

I disconnect the call as I round the corner for my street. Pulling into the driveway, I press the garage opener and park inside. Just as I exit the car, Skylar arrives. I gesture for her to pull beside me. With all the bullshit going on, the last thing either of us needs is a vandalized vehicle.

We share a brief kiss before I close the garage and we enter the house. I want to tell her about the woman at the store. Tell her about the supposed evidence. But she had a shitty day. Do I really want to make it worse?

Not like there is a choice.

I empty the grocery sack and get to work on dinner. Skylar offers to cut the potatoes and start the pasta water. After pounding out the chicken, I coat the breasts in parmesan and add them to the oven with the potatoes. I chop some broccoli to cook with the pasta and set them aside until it's time.

Taking a deep breath, I lean back on the counter and hold Skylar's gaze. "So, I need to tell you something."

"Okay." She draws out the word and my insides twist in a knot.

"Someone is definitely messing with us."

Skylar tips her head to the side and studies my expression. "How do you know?" She asks as if she suspects as much, but isn't one-hundred-percent sold.

"The whispers, the accounts at work, your flat tire. Also, at the store, my card got declined at checkout shortly after a woman lipped off and said she saw 'evidence' of what I did to Kelli."

Skylar's eyes go wide. "What evidence?"

I shrug. "Don't know. She didn't give details. But she made her disgust obvious."

Panicked, Skylar whips her phone from a pocket,

unlocks it, and taps rapidly on the screen. I open my mouth to say something. To tell her it will be okay. That we will get through this. But I don't. Instead, I shut my mouth and drop the pasta in the water. I flip the chicken and stir the potatoes. Doing these things is better than telling Skylar everything will be fine.

Because I have no clue how this will play out. Have no clue if we will end up further tarnished and, if so, to what degree.

"Oh my god," Skylar says on a gasp. She claps her hand to her mouth. "Oh. My. God." Her skin goes impossibly paler.

"What?"

Eyes wide and glassy, she stumbles to my side, hand trembling as she passes me her phone.

On the screen—*on fucking YouTube*—is a seven minute and twenty-one second video of me and Skylar. In my kitchen. Fucking on the counter. My back to the camera. Most of her profile hidden by her hair and my face. But it is there.

Right. Fucking. There. For anyone and everyone to watch.

Immediately, I drop my eyes to the number of views, likes, and shares. A dozen views. No likes and two dislikes. Zero shares.

Thank fuck.

I pull the video up on my phone. "Report the video for sexual content," I tell her. "I'll do the same."

The fact there is a video of us online is one-hundred-percent shitty. But at least the numbers are low. With only a dozen views, the damage isn't widespread. I would rather people gossip than see this video. Gossip can be dispelled. Videos are a wholly different beast.

This beast needs to be removed. Now.

The biggest problem either of us face... getting the video from the original source.

Kelli.

Surely, she saved the video on her phone. Fingers crossed the only place she shared it is YouTube.

Unfortunately, I now have a new problem to talk with Glen about. The situation much more personal, but I need to ask if any other measures need to be taken. Until then, we tackle it head-on, the only way we know how, through the proper channels. YouTube won't tell Kelli who reported it. Just that it was reported and removed.

If we get lucky, they will flag and monitor her account for similar future activity.

Most of dinner passes in silence. Neither of us harbors anger for the other, but a storm cloud of irritation and frustration looms above.

And it pisses me off.

Who the hell does she think she is? Sure, the Langston name holds some prestige in Stone Bay. But her entitlement doesn't give her a free pass to do whatever the hell she pleases.

Was what Kelli did wrong? Hell, yes. But Skylar and I were no innocents in this either.

Although I broke up with Kelli more times than I can

count on two hands, she clung to me harder than a gibbon monkey to its mate. Some may call it loyalty. I call it annoying as fuck. No matter how firm or kind I had been with each breakup announcement, Kelli blew it off. Laughed as if I had been joking.

Kelli Langston needs help. The help only licensed professionals offer. But how do we make that happen? How do we prove Kelli is behind all this?

As if my questions were broadcasted via satellite, my phone vibrates in my pocket. I retrieve it to see Glen's name on the screen.

"Who is it?" Skylar asks, picking at her meal too.

"Answers, I hope." I tap the green icon on the screen. "Your ears ringing, man?"

"Only until you answered." Glen chuckles. "Wanted to call with an update. You sitting down?"

My fork slips from my fingers and clangs against the stoneware. I wince, not realizing it had still been in my hand.

Three words.

You sitting down?

How did three simple words laced together send a chill up my spine?

Glen had been digging for hours. After my lunch with Terrance, I asked him to look into the additional missing money. At first, I thought he would need access to Terrance's computer. Turns out, it wasn't necessary. So long as we used the same servers, he could access Terrance's history via my computer. The process made it less noticeable to anyone snooping. Glen had said, "If anyone asks, just say your computer was making strange noises." End of story.

"Why do I not like the sound of this?"

He huffs on the other end. "Because it's not good, man. Sorry."

I rest an elbow on the table and drop my head in my hand. Take a deep breath. Then another. And another.

If Glen says this isn't good, it's *bad*. The dreadful kind of bad.

"Lay it on me, man."

"It's someone in-house. Took a lot to unearth answers, but I located the source." He pauses, giving us both a moment to register his revelation. "I don't have a name, just a user ID. But they've been skimming accounts for years. Whoever it is, they're damn good at covering their tracks. Tech smart. Or knows someone who is."

I sag into the chair, pinching the bridge of my nose. "Jesus."

"After I traced down your issue, I checked your coworker's computer. Same user ID. Once I nailed those down, on a whim, I decided to dig deeper. Look at all the activity for this user."

Don't mind me, while I have a heart attack, waiting for Glen to finish after his dramatic pause. "And?"

"And whoever this is, they've been at it a long damn time. More than a decade."

The first thought to cross my mind—it's not Terrance. He hit his ten-year mark two months ago. Busted his ass for the accolades framed on his office walls. Worked hard to make a name for himself in Stone Bay.

One thing not his forte… technology.

Terrance knew how to navigate the company software. Spent extra time with training to understand the program, so as to not look the fool with clients. But if I ask him to create a spreadsheet with pie charts, he pawns the task off on his assistant.

Aside from me, there are only three others with tenure exceeding a decade. Garrett, Sheila, and Theodore.

January third, there had been a cake in the staff break room, large two and zero candles plunged in the frosting. Sheila's cheeks had been tight and red the entire day from smiling. Her husband and daughter, in on the surprise celebration, showered her with a bundle of wildflowers and half a dozen colorful balloons.

Sheila is a pillar in the community. Many women, young and old, look up to her. Listen to her personal story when she talks about saving and growing for the future. Sheila didn't grow up in poverty, but she understands hardship. With each rough patch in her past, she trudged through and came out on the other side stronger.

Which is why I know it isn't Sheila.

Theodore Osborn is respected as much as the Stone Bay original families. Such merits don't come easily in a small town, but Ted earned the honor through decades of hard work. He also founded Stone Bay Financial. Built it from the ground up. Established trust with the residents that he would keep their wealth safe.

Thirty-seven years.

Ted founded the only investment business in town thirty-seven years ago. When I was in training under-pants and breaking my thumb-sucking habit. No matter which angle I look at the situation from, it is impossible to picture Ted embezzling client money. He sacrificed too much. No way he would hand himself a one-way ticket to prison. No way he would ruin his future and that of his wife, children, and grandchildren.

Which leaves one other person.

Someone I trust.

Trusted.

Garrett Dunn.

But why? Why ruin your entire life over money? Sure, in the beginning, seeing all those numbers, the temptation tipped the scale. Then reason kicked in. Why tarnish your future so completely?

By no means am I a saint. I have committed my share of sin. Hell, I just had a sex video removed from YouTube. A video where I knowingly *cheated* on a woman who thought we were in a relationship. Yes, I tried terminating the relationship like a gentleman several times. But the break up never stuck.

So, I took harsh, drastic measures.

Do I regret *cheating* on Kelli? Not for a second. Could I have taken another tactic? Probably, but it would have perpetuated the cycle.

And I was done.

Tipping my head back, I stare unfocused at the ceiling. I don't want to ask, but need to hear the truth.

"Glen, what's the user ID?"

He prattles off a mix of letters and numbers. A combination I memorized after seeing it countless times over the years.

I hang my head and close my eyes. Dinner churns in my stomach, threatening to make an appearance. Slowly, methodically, I take a deep breath. More follow. They don't vanquish the disgust in my veins, but they calm my stomach slightly.

"You know who that is?" Glen asks.

Unfortunately. "Yeah." I clutch my forehead. "Any way you can send me a report of findings? I need evidence to take the next step."

"No problem. I'll have it in your inbox by morning."

"Appreciate your help, man. And, Glen?"

"Yes?"

"Mind sending the report to my personal email. Just in case."

"Sure thing."

The call disconnects and the list of things to do grows longer as I stare at the last of my dinner.

Fuck, fuck, fuck.

Guess I won't get much sleep tonight.

FIFTEEN

SKYLAR

A LOUD CRACK rips through the house seconds before the blare of the house alarm.

I bolt upright in bed, tug the sheet to my chest, and notice Lawrence missing. His side of the bed cold when I press my palm to the cotton. Muttered speech echoes from down the hall, followed by the crunch of higher-pitched gravel as the alarm quiets.

"Law," I whisper into the dark room. No answer.

Fumbling through the dark, I locate my clothes and don them. I tiptoe to the bedroom door, turn the knob, and crack it enough to peek out. Darkness and a hint of light greets me from downstairs. Inhaling deeply, I creep to the top landing, stay in the shadows, and spy on the first floor.

Before I whisper for Lawrence again, he ascends the stairs. I start for him, but he holds up a hand to stop me.

"What's going on? Are you okay?" I blurt. My eyes

roam his face in search of injury, but come up empty. Thank goodness.

He frames my face with his hands and I exhale my held breath. "I'm fine, little phoenix." His lips press mine in a gentle kiss. "The foyer window, on the other hand, is not."

I open my mouth, prepared to ask a grocery list of questions, but he captures my lips once more. This kiss is not gentle or sweet. Lawrence packs this kiss with a one-two-three punch. Steals the breath from my lungs. Snakes his arms around my frame and seizes my ass in his hands. A moan spills from my lips and he swallows it whole. My fingers fist his shirt and pull the hem from his trousers. Then my nails skate up his back.

Which is the exact moment he pulls away.

He rests his forehead on mine, breath heavy and desperate. Eyes pinched tight. He grips my hips, his fingers digging at the flesh beneath my clothes.

"Shoes," he mutters, breath hot on my lips. "Put on shoes. There's glass everywhere."

I lift a hand and comb my fingers through his hair. Relish his weight as he leans into my touch. "What happened?"

"Someone threw a hammer at the foyer window." Holy. Shit. "Looks like there's something attached. The police are on the way."

This has Kelli Langston written all over it. Conniving. Deceitful. Petty.

Maybe it is the same hammer that drove a nail in my tire.

Yes, Law and I did something heinous by staging the kitchen sex for her to walk in on. In her eyes, Lawrence committed the ultimate relationship crime. Cheating. Had anyone else found out prior to her sharing the video, the town wouldn't just be whispering about me and Law. She and the Langston family would be tarnished for generations to come.

So, this must be her revenge. Posting vulnerable videos online. Spreading rumors to paint herself as the brokenhearted woman dragged through the mud and abandoned on the roadside. Kelli will never tell the story of Lawrence breaking up with her countless times prior to that night. A story like that won't garner the level of sympathy her ego needs. And surely, no one breaks up with Kelli Langston—at least, that is probably how she and half the town see it.

Flashes of red and blue light the lower staircase. Lawrence kisses me briefly on the lips, then tucks a wayward strand of hair behind my ear as he takes a step down.

"Put shoes on. Be careful when you come down." A heavy sigh leaves his lips. "It's going to be a long night."

Tangerine and indigo paint the altocumulus clouds above the bay. A soft daffodil yellow beneath the pillowy puffs. As if the sky couldn't decide what to do this morning. Staring at the skyline, I decide it is broken. But not as broken as I am right now.

After hours of questions, crime scene photos, and a temporary fix to the window, my bones ache. My muscles are weary. The earth could open up and swallow me whole right now, and I wouldn't care. I am just... tired. Exhausted. Twenty-four-hours-of-straight-sleep-wouldn't-help tired.

But I refuse to admit defeat. Refuse to surrender to someone who works for nothing and gets everything.

Well, guess what, bitch? You won't win this one.

Warm arms wrap around my middle, tug me close, imprison me physically and emotionally. My body sags against his frame. Let's go and allows him to hold me upright. "There you are," he whispers at the shell of my ear, breath warm on my skin. His arms cradle me tighter. "Got worried when I couldn't find you."

Lawrence kisses beneath my ear, his lips painting desire down the side of my neck. He stops where my neck and shoulder meet. Pays more attention with tongue and teeth before he climbs back up, turns my head, and captures my lips with his.

I get lost in the kiss. In his hands roaming my body. In the taste of him on my tongue. When his hand dips between my waistband and skin, I break the kiss. Not

because I don't want this to go further. But because we
need to talk.

Lawrence and I aren't just sex. Okay, maybe ninety-
five percent sex. As they say, don't mess with a good thing.

Regardless, we need to talk about what happened
tonight. Last night. This morning. Whatever the hell it was.
We need to talk about Kelli and how to proceed. And without
breaking confidentiality, we need to talk about his work.

"I'm okay, Law." I lay a peck on his cheek. "If we
didn't have such pressing matters to discuss, I'd let you
take me here, out in the open." I twist in his arms and
peek up at him. "But we really should talk."

He deflates faster than my overly duct-taped camping
air mattress. His arms untangle from my body; the fingers
of one hand finding mine. "Come here."

Guiding us to the lounger on the patio, he straddles
the seat, sits, then pulls me between his legs. Ten full
breaths pass, our eyes fixed on the brightening sky before
he locates his voice.

"Cops weren't able to lift prints from the hammer, note
or pictures. Luckily, I have cameras installed on the
house." There are cameras on the house? Even this information is news to me. He rubs his palms up and down my
biceps. "I had them installed when I bought the house, but
have never told anyone. They're small—discreet. But this
was my first house, and I wanted to protect what's mine."

"Makes sense," I say, relaxing under his touch.

"Didn't intentionally not tell you. Just habit. Hell, I've

never had a reason to review them, so I forget they're installed."

Shifting, I rest my head on the front of his shoulder and rotate my head slightly. Take in his stubbled jawline, thicker than usual. Tempting. But I shut down my thirsty brain.

"Were they able to get anything from the cameras?"

Behind me, Lawrence shrugs. "I pulled up the feed on the computer, but had to email the video. Whoever threw the hammer, I don't know how, but they knew where the cameras were. Knew where to stay in the shadows. So, the cops are using their resources to try and lighten the frames."

If Lawrence never told anyone about the cameras, the person must have cased his house. Visited on other occasions and scoped out the place. Much as I hate Kelli, I don't think she has the wherewithal to execute such a task.

Or does she?

Not that a Langston has the need to rob or blackmail. I don't know their wealth status, but I would venture to guess there is more than one comma in their bank accounts.

No diss against my boyfriend, but why would Kelli be so adamant about staying with Lawrence?

He broke it off several times, yet she kept him on a short leash. Didn't let him move on. Why? She doesn't strike me as overly affectionate. I'd bet my savings there isn't a romantic bone in her body.

So, again... why?

"Theories are running circles in my head," I tell Lawrence.

He kisses my temple. "Like what? At this point, I'm open to all possibilities."

"Before we started seeing each other, nothing outlandish happened to either of us."

His head bops side to side. "True."

"Us dating interrupted someone's plan."

"Plan?"

"Not sure what the plan is, but the change pissed someone off." I lay my hand over his. "Kelli may be a part of said plan, but I don't think she's the mastermind. She doesn't pull the strings. I think Kelli was just a distraction. Someone to divert your attention." The more I say aloud, the more sense it makes. "Why else would she not let you go?" I twist to face him better. "Not that I'll ever let you go." I laugh. "But you broke it off how many times? A woman like Kelli would take rejection, smear it with a new beau, and flaunt her happiness in your face." Lawrence stares off into the distance, eyes glazed over. "Tell me I'm wrong and I'll drop it."

The sun rises in the skyline, the clouds shifting and dissipating. Meanwhile, Lawrence absorbs my theory. Mulls over it from every angle. Brows pinching, then widening, then pinching again.

I don't know his exact thoughts, but if I were him, I would be hurt. Not only is the woman who he dated going off her rocker, but things at work are in shambles too.

Which reminds me...

"Did you get the details from Glen?"

Blinking away the fog, his eyes drop to mine and he nods. "Yeah. I was looking it over when everything happened. Hadn't gotten far, but it's not looking good." His head tips back and rests on the lounger, a heavy sigh on his lips. "I need to call Ted. Talk with him face to face. Tell him what I found. Then, we need to fix this. Fast." His eyes close as he lifts a hand to pinch the bridge of his nose. "Before the news gets out an employee embezzled client money. *Fuck*."

This isn't just bad. It is an epic pile of elephant shit.

What I don't get is how this is all connected. Because it has to be. No way these incidents—his work and all the crazy shit that has happened to us both since we got together—don't tie together with a pretty bow. Question is, how?

Wish I had the answers. Until they are in my hand, I refuse to stop digging. Until I have answers, Kelli Langston has a new stalker on her hands.

Game on, bitch.

SIXTEEN

LAWRENCE

WHAT IS WORSE than calling your boss to ask for a private, undisclosed meeting? Seeing him outside when you pull into his driveway, arms crossed over his chest, jaw clenched and mouth in a straight line.

Theodore Osborn doesn't have an intimidating bone in his body. It is a rare occasion to not see a smile on his face. He volunteers at the food bank and donates to charities for families and children. The man has done more good in the last five years than I have done in my entire adult life.

Theodore Osborn may be a spectacular human—forgiving and gentle and kind—but I don't picture him reacting well to a thief in the company. *His company.*

I sure as hell wouldn't.

File folder in hand, I exit the car and take the path to his porch steps. Sweat slicks my brow in the fifteen-foot distance. My shirt constricts my chest and arms. And with each breath I take, the air thins. Although I am not the guilty party, I hate bearing this news to a man who is nothing but wonderful to everyone he meets.

"Hey, Ted. Sorry about the weird call, but you'll understand in a minute."

He offers his hand and we shake. "You wouldn't ask to meet like this if it wasn't important. Doesn't mean I like it, but I respect the discretion."

Ted leads us inside, pours us each water, and shows me to his living room. I sip the water, set the glass down, take a deep breath, then dive headfirst into Ted's biggest nightmare.

Once I finished reading Glen's report, something else didn't add up.

Although Garrett's user ID was all over the transactions, it felt too easy. Almost sloppy. Garrett fit the profile for the time frame, but nothing else matches. If I don't question the nagging in my gut, I may as well point the finger without undeniable evidence.

Garrett is a smart man. Has worked with Ted seventeen years. Is well known in the community and loved by those he works with. He gives back to the community and helps old ladies put groceries in their car.

Why would Garrett steal thousands of dollars?

The man is no millionaire, but he earns more than most dream of. More than me, and my pay is substantial.

So, I started looking at the situation as if I didn't know anyone. Stopped letting my history with each person sway my opinion. And that is when a few things clicked in place, but not all. My hope is Ted helps connect the rest.

I lay the folder on the table as I finish the catastrophic news. Ted hangs his head, rests his elbows on his knees, then flexes and relaxes his fingers over and over. The tops of his ears grow redder with each jagged breath he takes.

Never has this man raised his voice. Never has he thrown something in anger. But right now, he looks capable of mass destruction.

Someone messed with what is his. Someone put his reputation and life at stake. And Ted... he is fucking pissed.

"Who knows what you've discovered?" he asks, meeting my eyes.

The sinister glint in his typically gentle eyes sends a chill down my spine. I shake my head. "You and me. No one else."

"Your friend." He gestures to the file. "What does he know?"

"He's a tech nerd. Numbers are all he knows. No names."

"You're certain?"

I lean forward and look Ted square in the eye. "I trust him with my life."

The room quiets for far too long. Ted stares at the folder, at the pile of documentation scattered over the table, at the figures any ethical person would vomit over had they caught it.

Ted sips his water, sits back, and stares out the window. "Here's what we're going to do..."

For the next half hour, Ted tells me his plan. We hash

out the finer details and discuss what to do if different scenarios come into play before the big hurrah. It isn't often Ted is in the thick of day-to-day activity at Stone Bay Financial, but that is only because he has other responsibilities. Seeing him like this, though, I imagine him being a force to reckon with years back.

I leave the file with him and head home. Over the weekend, I plan to do a little side digging of my own. Scour the internet for anything we missed or didn't give attention to years ago.

Lawrence: Headed home. What's your ETA?

While I went to talk with Ted, Skylar went into the office to make up lost hours from the day of the flat tire.

Skylar: Leaving in ten. Yours or mine?
Lawrence: Yours. Mine is a mess. I'll grab clothes and meet you soon. Food?
Skylar: A BBQ double bacon cheeseburger, onion rings and a shake from the diner sounds perfect.
Lawrence: Think I'll get the same. See you in a bit.
Skylar: Mwah!

Parked in the driveway, I dash in the house, pack a duffel for the weekend, grab my laptop, then call in an order at the diner. I walk room to room and check all the windows are locked. Check every entry point to make sure the bolts are securely in place. Once the alarm is set, I jump in the car and drive to the diner.

Relaxing this weekend sounds heavenly. Me, Skylar, takeout, snacks, and television. Perfect.

Unfortunately, if the unwelcome pang beneath my diaphragm has a say in the matter, there won't be any relaxing moments until this whole mess ends.

Hopefully, this all comes to a close soon. If all goes according to plan, the guilty party will be behind bars in no time.

SEVENTEEN

SKYLAR

Holy. Shit.

I blink, then stare at the screen with narrowed eyes. Zoom to two hundred percent, then narrow my eyes again. The image turns grainy, but I have zero doubts about who is on the screen.

Kelli Bitchface Langston.

But it isn't just her. Nope. That bitch is lip-locked with some guy. Terrance Marshall. This is his social media account, after all. And the profile picture looks like an older version of the guy in this photo.

Delilah told me to dig deep, so that is what I did.

Kelli's social media is public and spotless. I expected nothing less. The last few hours have been a mix of work catch-up and internet searches. Too much time was spent on Kelli's accounts. I had no expectations but hoped for a nugget of information.

Nada.

So, I moved onto a generic internet search. Typed her name in the search engine and siphoned through an endless stream of results. Articles from the Stone Bay Gazette depicting the Langston family over the years. Pageant photos from her childhood. High school yearbook pictures.

Three pages of results in and I was ready to give up. Nothing fruitful had shown itself. But I said *one more page,* and it paid off. At least, I think it will.

I adjust the zoom back to normal and print what I found. It is the only picture I found on Terrance's profile with Kelli, but maybe it is enough. God, I hope so.

"Shit," I mutter after seeing the time. Lawrence will be at the house any minute.

I shove the printout in my purse, shut down my computer, and wind my way out of the office. Fob in hand, I push through the door and dart for the car. A light drizzle coats my skin and cools the summer heat.

A quick press of the fob and tug of the handle, I open the door and hop in, pressing the ignition. Music blares from the speakers as I riffle through my purse for my phone and type out a quick text to Lawrence.

Skylar: Leaving now. Be there in 5.

Might be more like seven or eight, unless I press the accelerator a little harder.

Lawrence: Just got here myself.

Thank goodness. I shove the phone back in my purse and toss it on the passenger seat. Buckling my belt, I throw the car in reverse and look in the rearview mirror. A set of bright-white teeth gleam back at me.

Before I open my mouth to scream, the world goes dark.

"Do you have any hot friends?" Kirsten asks as we wait for Skylar to get home.

There isn't an occasion I remember feeling intimidated by a woman, but Kirsten definitely comes on strong. Even in general conversation. I mean, she is skirting around flattery so as to not intrude on her friend's relationship. But this whole conversation has been weird. Mainly because I don't look at my friends and think *he's hot*, or *she's hot*.

Maybe women do that, but most men I know don't. Not saying there aren't the occasional ones who do. They are out there, they just aren't my friends.

"Uh, maybe?" I answer with uncertainty.

Where's Skylar?

I glance down at my watch. She should have been here ten minutes ago. Even with wiggle room, she wouldn't be this late. I pull my phone from my pocket and tap the screen. No new messages.

Kirsten carries on about never meeting a hot guy at the pub. I listen enough to catch the occasional word, but otherwise don't absorb what she says.

Lawrence: Almost here?

I hit send and hope the text doesn't come across as pushy.

Yes, I have a stern demeanor. But Skylar brings out my softer side on occasion. With her, I balance the bold and rough with the tender and gentle.

Right now, with all this bullshit going on, Skylar not arriving on time, or close to, is worrisome.

My shoe slaps the tile, my eyes locked on the sent message.

Slap, slap, slap.

The phone screen dims and I tap it awake. Stare at it impatiently. No answer. No sign she has read the message. No little dancing bubble to indicate her typing or talking to text.

Lawrence: I'm worried, LP. Let me know you're okay.

The time at the top left of the screen mocks me as the minutes continue to advance.

Still. No. Response.

Bile slithers up my throat and I bite back the urge to vomit.

Lawrence: Just tell me you're okay. Please, Sky.

The magic gray bubble pops up. It dances and dances. Kirsten blathers on. At this point, I have no idea if she realizes I am not paying attention to her or she doesn't care. Either way, I refuse to look away from the bubble.

"Motherfucker!" I yell when the text hits my phone.

Kirsten stops talking, but her eyes burn holes through my skin. "What's wrong?" Her voice soft and shaky.

My eyes refuse to leave the screen. Refuse to look away from the image. Refuse to believe what I am looking at is real. But after everything that has happened, deep down, I know this nightmare is as real as it gets. And someone took Skylar.

At this point, I don't know if it is Terrance or Kelli or some other sick fuck. My eyes rake over her body in the photo. Wrists and ankles bound and strapped to an old metal bed frame. Burlap over her head, the length of her fiery curls peeking out. Clothes still in place, but tattered. The only thing I am unable to make out from the still is if she is conscious.

Two words sit below the image in the text history.

Call me.

Feels like hours passed since I last acknowledged Kirsten. I peer up from my phone, the room blurry.

"Someone took Skylar." She blinks a few times, my

words not quite sinking in. I flip my phone around and flash her the photo. "Someone. Took. Skylar," I say with more gusto.

A hand flies to her mouth. Tears flooding her eyes. "Oh my god." The words barely audible on her lips.

"Kirsten." She blinks and shifts her gaze, the tears painting parallel lines down her cheeks. "I need to call her phone. While I do that, I need you to go into a different room and call the police." She doesn't respond, only continues to stare blankly at the wall over my shoulder. "Kirsten, please."

One, two, three blinks and she shakes her head. "Yeah. Yes, I'll call. What do I say?"

"Tell them your roommate was on her way home. You and her boyfriend have been waiting at the house. He got a text with a photo and message to call. Describe the photo." I show it to her once more. "I'll try to drag it out as long as possible and get whatever details I can."

"Okay." Kirsten darts down the hall and steps into her bedroom.

I take a few steadying breaths, then tap the call icon under Skylar's profile name. On the second ring, the call connects and an all too familiar voice fills the line.

"Took you long enough. Hope you're not planning to be heroic."

Of course, I plan to be heroic. Just not in the way he thinks. I put the call on speaker and type out a new text while I talk.

"Not like I know where you are, Terrance. What I do know is if you hurt her, I will end you."

The quiet, somewhat introverted man I have known a decade laughs on the other end. The sound hollow and monstrous. "Like to see you try."

I finish the text and hit send. "Terrance, I don't make idle threats. I make promises." Kirsten tiptoes into the room and I press a finger to my lips. She shows me her phone screen, her call still active. "What is it you want, Terrance?"

"What, your tech friend didn't find all the answers?" He clicks his tongue. "Consider me surprised."

"Still not an answer."

"Pretty bold for someone who's not in charge, aren't you?" The line goes silent a moment. I clamp my jaw tight, and pain shoots through my molars. "You just couldn't leave well enough alone, could you? Had to mess everything up."

"What does that mean, Terrance?"

A muffled groan echoes in the background of the call, followed by a woman's voice muttering, "Shut up, stupid bitch."

My blood boils to the surface, lighting my skin on fire. Low or loud, I would know that voice anywhere. Kelli Langston. Hard as it is, I suffocate the urge to call her out.

"Mess what up, Terrance? I haven't done shit."

My phone vibrates with a new text and I tap the message. *Keep them talking.* I quickly respond. *On it.*

"You getting with this juvenile bitch ruined everything. I had it all mapped out. For years, it'd all been so smooth. No one noticed a damn thing. Everyone just said the market was fluctuating. That's always been the reason for the occasional dip in accounts. You just never noticed until last time. When I skimmed and then a stock took a major hit the next day."

Maybe because I don't think like a criminal, I am not connecting all the dots. If the market dipped, the numbers would have changed across the portfolio. Not in only one place. Terrance doesn't need to be privy to my lack of felonious mindset, though.

"I don't get you, man. You have it all. Why do this? Why fuck up your life?"

My phone vibrates with another text, this one with an image and address. I forward it to Kirsten and she dashes back to her room.

"I didn't fuck up shit. If you played nice, if you didn't keep trying to throw Kelli in the trash, everything would've stayed as it should be."

Kelli? Why the hell would Terrance care if I stayed with Kelli?

Yes, I heard her a moment ago. Yes, I assumed she played a role in some of the shit happening. Not with the money, but definitely the rumor mill and possibly the flat tire. There was no concrete evidence, though.

"Not wanting a relationship with someone is not throwing them in the trash. It's called life. Not everyone is compatible." I huff out a breath and pace the call. Speak slow and pray the cops get to Skylar quick. "I broke up with Kelli—over and over—because we had nothing in common. Because I wanted more out of life than a fake woman with a trust fund on my arm. Thought you knew me better."

"You piece of—"

A loud bang cuts Kelli off. Voices in the background scream, "Police! Get on the ground! Now!"

Kirsten runs out of her room, looks me in the eye, and we both dart for the front door. She disconnects the call with the police, but I leave the call with Skylar's phone open. I zip through town, pausing at stop signs and red lights long enough to not cause an accident. A mile out from the address, the call disconnects.

My heart bangs violently in my rib cage, begging for freedom. I bear down on the accelerator. Watch the speedometer needle crank clockwise, more and more.

"She'll be okay, Law," Kirsten says, resting a hand on my forearm. Her words meant to soothe both of us.

Flashing lights come into view and my heart calms slightly. I slam on the brakes and we jump out of the car. Running toward the house, I skid to a stop when the one voice I want to hear calls my name.

"Law." My head twists toward the ambulance.

Skylar.

My little phoenix.

Thank God.

NINETEEN

SKYLAR

Fear changes a person. Reshapes the way they see the world. How they look at and listen to people.

After what happened, everyone I see has a new face. A new aura. Sure, it will probably soften with time. But not for a while.

My abduction last month also changed Lawrence.

A new gentleness lives in him. As does a fierce protector. Combine them together and mix them with the blunt force that knocked me out before my abduction, and it equals Lawrence's fear. That someone or something else will hurt me.

Including sex.

Desperate as I am to have him, I don't push for more than his body spooning mine at night. Lawrence has had a full plate since the showdown. The web of deceit was much larger than we knew, but came to light within hours.

Terrance and Kelli may have been my abductors, but they weren't the sole captors.

After the police pummeled the front door, a frenzy ensued—and I saw none of it. The sack over my head kept me in the dark until an officer freed my arms and legs.

The third person was a stranger. No one I had seen around town or spoken with in the past. Then the officers read each of them their Miranda rights and the name Garrett floated through the air. Immediately, my heart sank for Lawrence. For the trust he had bestowed upon these men over the years. Trust they exploited with each cent they embezzled.

But it wasn't just Terrance and Garrett. Kelli had been equally guilty.

Kelli and Garrett had known each other since grade school. Although Garrett's family wasn't as financially well off as Kelli's, they ran in similar circles. They had never publicly dated but had been an item since high school. When Kelli's great-grandfather passed away, her parents denied her the money left to her in his will since she was still a minor. Instead, they put the money in a trust. Set stipulations and year markers as to when she would receive money.

Needless to say, Kelli was pissed.

Early in college, Kelli convinced Garrett to help her steal money from her parents. Cash from the home safe every now and again. Stealing family jewelry and pawning it out of state. Online purchases with credit cards the parents didn't study line by line.

But it hadn't been enough.

Kelli knew she had millions collecting dust. Millions her parents wouldn't give her until she married. Which is where Lawrence came into play. Kelli plotted out her relationship with Lawrence, an upstanding man in Stone Bay that many looked up to. Clung to him in the hopes they would marry with a prenup, she would collect her money, then divorce and run off with Garrett.

Why she didn't just marry Garrett... we still haven't figured that one out. Maybe they didn't want to be legally connected. Maybe Kelli sees him more as fun and not permanent. Perhaps the conniving bitch wanted to keep her options open.

And Terrance.

Where does Terrance fit in?

Garrett recruited Terrance. Found him through a hacker site. Convinced him he would get a pretty penny if he helped out. The payoff wouldn't be immediate, but they'd be set for life. As a bonus, Garrett *shared* Kelli with Terrance.

The three of them were one big mindfuck.

But since all this came to light, Lawrence and his boss, along with a few other employees, have been scrambling to fix the mess. Hours of records sifted through by a few trusted staff, the company's tech guy, and Lawrence's friend, Glen. The loss of at least six figures has been a disaster, but they are righting all the wrongs and involving the impacted clients.

Which means Lawrence has been busier than usual and we have had less *us* time.

But that changes tonight.

Although fiercely protective of my every move, I convinced Lawrence the threat of danger passed. Convinced him to go to work and leave me on my own.

His house, since the window repair, has become a fortress. Additional security measures, including a passcode gate at the front of the property and a dozen more cameras, have been put in place.

Reluctantly, he caved to my pleas for solitude, but only had a few requests.

One—if I were alone during the day, I stayed at his place.

Two—I was not to let anyone on the property I didn't know.

Three—most importantly—let him know when I leave and arrive from places.

Some may say Lawrence's behavior is a bit much. Possessive versus protective. I tell them to shut the hell up.

If the man I love asks me to do these things so he knows I am safe, I choose to follow through. It isn't daunting. It doesn't diminish who I am.

I am my own woman. Make my own choices. But there is nothing wrong with, from time to time, letting my man take the helm. He loves my fire and insatiable hunger as much as I love his dominance and voracious need. It is a give and take for both of us.

The gate buzzer echoes throughout the house and I dash to the keypad by the door.

"Hello?"

"Grocery delivery for York."

"Be right there."

I slip on shoes and jog down the driveway.

Preincident, I would've opened the door to anyone. Now, not so much.

I meet the delivery guy at the gate and wave thank you as he drives off. I collect the bags, take them inside, and get to work.

Tonight, I aim to quell Lawrence's fear. Tonight, I want this man to resurrect his little phoenix.

TWENTY

LAWRENCE

THE HOUSE IS dark when I open the door. Only a flicker lights the way.

"Skylar?" I call out as I enter the house from the garage.

"In the kitchen."

In the dark, the kitchen feels a mile away. I kick off my shoes and pad across the floor to the kitchen. A lone tea light candle lights the space, but I don't see her.

Panic floods my bloodstream as I scan the room. The few heart pounding seconds end when I spot her on the counter, off to the side. Naked.

Holy hell.

The zipper of my pants digs at my flesh as I take her in. My heart racing for an entirely different reason now.

More than a month has passed since I was last inside my girl. Since her warmth enveloped me and brought me to my knees.

Tonight, I make amends.

Like a jaguar hunting prey, I take measured steps in her direction. Run my fingertips along the edge of the island counter. Lick my lips as I rake my eyes over her exposed flesh.

"What's my little phoenix been up to today?"

I stop a foot away. Eager as I am to take her, the foreplay will make it so much better when I do.

She hums, lifts a hand to the top of her sternum, then trails her fingers down her midline until they land between her thighs. Once, twice, three times, she circles her clit. She props one foot on the counter and spreads her legs wider.

Sweet fucking Christ.

"I made dinner." Skylar *is* dinner. "And dessert." She circles her fingers again before they disappear inside her.

And I can't fucking take it anymore.

Erasing the distance between us, I claim her mouth and undo my pants. Trace the head of my cock up and down her slick entrance. Scoot her ass closer to the edge and push inside her.

A guttural moan rips through the air. Her nails dig at my biceps, her breath hot on my neck. Too much time has passed since we were like this. Wild and feral and desperate.

I worried she wouldn't want me after what happened. Not just physically, but in any capacity. For years, I worked alongside two of the three who hurt her. And I knew *nothing*.

Guilt racked me day and night. Stole hours of precious sleep. Haunted me every waking minute as I worked tirelessly to fix the problems at Stone Bay Financial.

Why would Skylar want me after everything? I couldn't picture her looking at me with the same heart-shaped eyes. Couldn't imagine her wanting to be with a man who fell victim to a major financial scheme. Something the townies would talk about for years.

Why would she trust me again? Had our roles been reversed, I may have questioned our shared trust. Although our connection is profound, our relationship is still so young.

So, I gave her space. Time to think without interruption. Time to decide without persuasion.

It seems she has decided.

My hips pick up the pace. Piston in and out faster. My mouth on her lips, her jaw, her neck, her nipple. Her sweet sounds grow in pitch. Come faster and louder as her orgasm builds. Then her walls clamp down. Vise grip my cock. I let go and come inside her.

I wrap her in my arms, hug her close to my chest. Her fingers comb through my hair as her ankles lock around my waist.

"I really did make dinner," she says.

Laughter spills from my lips and I press a kiss to her hair before leaning back to see her face. I cup one cheek, then the other, and lock onto her gaze. "I love you, Skylar."

Her eyes glaze over as her chin wobbles. "I love you,

too." She presses a chaste kiss to my lips. "But I much rather you call me little phoenix."

The corner of my mouth curves up. "Love you, little phoenix. Forever." I kiss the tip of her nose. "Now, what's for dinner?"

Nails scrape down my back until she palms my ass. "Let's have dessert first."

Skylar York will forever be my favorite dessert. "Anything you want, little phoenix, it's yours. I'm yours."

EPILOGUE

SKYLAR

Three months later

GOSSIP OVER THE KELLI, Garrett, and Terrance situation is finally on a low simmer. But you better believe the entire town had the nationally broadcasted trial on television. No matter what food establishment or store you walked into two weeks ago, the trial was on for all to see.

Garrett and Kelli had been sentenced more harshly than Terrance. Between the three of them, they would be paying hefty fines and flaunting orange behind bars for decades to come.

Since their heinous crimes came to light, the town gossip mill cared less about me and Lawrence.

Thank God.

"I'm ordering pizza," Kirsten shouts from the living room. "Any requests?"

Puffing out a breath, the loose strands from my ponytail float up and then fall back to my cheeks. My stomach groans for some form of sustenance. Anything. Grabbing another large trash bag, I meander to my open bedroom door, poke my head into the hall, and shake the bag open.

"Hawaiian for me and supreme for Law."

"Dr Pepper?"

My brows pinch together. "Is that a real question?"

Laughter travels down the hall as I step back into my room and head for the closet. Bag open, I shove several hangers loaded with tops together and bag them while they still hang, tying the bag ends near the hooks. I do this several times until every item hanging in my closet is makeshift dress bags.

Exiting the closet, my eyes travel around the room. A bedroom I called mine for the past three years. A bedroom that will soon be vacant. My eyes sting as they take in the bare walls. My throat swells with emotion as I stare at the bed, now covered in boxes, where some of my favorite chats happened with my best friends.

God, I will miss Kirsten and Delilah. Miss the girl time we get without effort. Miss the comfort of having my best friends a room away. The laughter, the tears, and the lack of judgment. But most importantly, the hugs and reassurances. These ladies... they are my soul sisters.

Eventually, we knew this day would come. The day one of us moves forward. Takes the next leg of our journey. Solo. Well, kind of solo.

Taking the next step is scary. And though we knew it was inevitable, we couldn't predict *when* it would occur.

On a random Friday evening two weeks ago, Lawrence went all out. Created a dinner chefs would fawn over. Lit dozens of candles. Presented me with a beautiful bouquet of wildflowers. Spoiled me with sweets and carbs. Made love to me until both of us couldn't walk straight lines.

And then, he asked me to move in.

Since the very beginning, our relationship has been a whirlwind. Before Lawrence, I never pictured myself with a man such as him. Strong and bold. Domineering yet gentle. Insatiable. But we just clicked.

Some say we won't last. That the difference in our ages will catch up. That his maturity will smother my spontaneity. That my naivety will rake his nerves. But those people know nothing about us. The real us.

Lawrence and I don't look at each other and see age or maturity level. We don't care what the general populace thinks or says about our relationship. The only thing of importance when it comes to us is that we love each other.

And god, do we love each other. With unparalleled ferocity.

So it wasn't difficult to say yes to Lawrence when he asked me to move in with him. Us becoming more is inevitable. Moving in after dating less than six months seems rash to outsiders. A juvenile move. But why delay what is destined to happen? Why wait?

As I empty the last dresser drawer of clothes and shove them in a box, louder conversation trickles down the hall. Seconds later, the conversation dies and I assume the pizza arrived. Wanting to finish the dresser items, I carry a small box over and place the items on top inside. Pictures of me with Kirsten and Delilah. Bead bracelets the three of us made one night when Kirsten had the urge to be crafty. The perfume Delilah bought me for Christmas. A small box that held the little bit of jewelry I owned. Cute sticky notes I saved. The mason jar candle Ollie got me for my twenty-second birthday.

Warm arms wrap around my waist as I close the flaps of the box. I melt into the familiar frame at my back. Inhale his sweet, earthy cologne. Close my eyes as I press my hips into his groin.

His lips drop to the skin where my neck and shoulder meet. A soft growl vibrates off him as his tongue darts out to taste me. His fingers curl tight on my hips as he works to stop my slow, sweet torture.

"Little phoenix," he says, warning in his tone. "You know I'd take you here and now if we didn't have other priorities."

Like moving my entire life into his house tonight.

Three nights ago, Lawrence asked how the packing had been coming along. Considering we both worked full-time and had been with each other every other minute of the day, he knew my answer. It hadn't been coming along. At all. And like the assertive man he is, he'd said, "All your belongings better be in my house, *our house*, by the weekend."

Seeing as today is Saturday and we have plans to go hiking tomorrow, moving day is today. No exception.

Thankfully, all the furniture is staying. Whoever moves in with Kirsten and Delilah won't have to worry about furnishings. All I have left to pack is my bathroom, which can easily be accomplished after we eat.

"Fine," I huff out. "But tonight—"

"You're mine," he says, cutting me off. "In *our* bed."

God, I love it when he says ours. Love the way the simple word rolls off his tongue and blankets my skin. Like another form of ownership. His ownership of me and my ownership of him. Now, though, we have an ours. And god, is it heady.

After I cross fold the box flaps, we join Kirsten in the living room for pizza, soda, and a rom-com she chose for us to watch. Two slices in, Delilah walks in the door. She drops her purse, kicks off her shoes, and joins us. Crossing her legs as she sits on the rug, she reaches for a slice of cheese, leans back and into my calf, and aims her eyes at the screen.

Just like that, my last night in this house feels perfect. With my friends close and the man I love at my side.

What an incredible life.

Although we won't be under the same roof, I will see Kirsten and Delilah often. For girls' nights and trips to the bookstore and movie nights at this house or mine. Texts and phone calls will occur more often. Chats about exciting new adventures. Advice on the next phase of our life. Because friendships don't get any tighter than the ones I share with these incredible women. Like it or not, they are stuck with me and I am stuck with them. Wouldn't have it any other way.

As the boxes empty and the movie ends, we shuffle in separate directions. Lawrence and I to my room. Kirsten to the kitchen to tidy up and Delilah to her room to change after a long day.

One box and bag at a time, we carry my belongings out. With each trip, I feel the change settle over me. The fact that this is no longer the place I call home.

"Ready?" Lawrence asks as he steps back into the house. The last of the boxes in our cars.

Taking a deep breath, I step over to Kirsten and Delilah. Hug them a little harder. Give them a soft smile as I retreat.

"Yeah." I have never been more ready.

MORE BY PERSEPHONE AUTUMN

The Click Duet

High school sweethearts torn apart. When fate gives them a second chance, one doesn't trust they won't be hurt again. Through the Lens (Click Duet #1) and Time Exposure (Click Duet #2) is an angsty, second chance, friends to lovers romance with all the feels.

The Inked Duet

A man with a broken heart and a woman scared to put herself out there. Love is never easy. Sometimes love rips you apart. Fine Line (Inked Duet #1) and Love Buzz (Inked Duet #2) is a second chance at love, single parent romance with a pinch of angst and dash of suspense.

The Insomniac Duet

He was her high school bully. She was the outcast that secretly crushed on him. More than ten years later, he's her boss, completely oblivious to their shared past, and wants no one but her. More importantly, he doesn't understand her animosity toward him.

The Artist Duet

A tortured hero with the biggest heart and a charismatic heroine with the patience of a saint. Previous heartache has him fighting his desire to be more than friends with her. But she is everywhere, and he can't help but give in. The Artist Duet is an angsty, friends to lovers slow burn.

Transcendental

A musician in search of his muse and a woman grieving the loss of her husband. Two weeks at an exclusive retreat and their connection rivals all others. Until she leaves early without notice. But he refuses to give up until he finds her again.

Distorted Devotion

Swept off her feet by love, life takes a dark, unexpected turn. Now the love of her life may be the cause of her death. Check out this gripping, romantic suspense.

Undying Devotion

A long-term couple with a secret life. Their friends envy the bond they share, but remain oblivious to their lifestyle and how deep the bond lies. A turn of events has her wanting to spill every secret.

Depths Awakened

A small town romance which captivates you from the start. Two broken souls have sworn off love. Vowed to never lose anyone else. But their undeniable attraction brings them together and refuses to let go.

THANK YOU

Thank you so much for reading **Broken Sky, the Stone Bay Series prequel**. If you wouldn't mind taking a moment to leave a review on the retailer site where you made your purchase, Goodreads and/or BookBub, it would mean the world to me.

Reviews help other readers find and enjoy the book as well.

Much love,
   Persephone

BROKEN SKY PLAYLIST

Here are some of the songs from the **Broken Sky** playlist.
You can listen to the entire playlist on Spotify!

First Glance | Zach Smith
Twisted | Two Feet
Animals | Sxint Prince
...Fuck | Johnny Rain
Psycho | Kevin Krokk
King | Niykee Heaton

Connect with Persephone

www.persephoneautumn.com

Subscribe to Persephone's Newsletter

www.persephoneautumn.com/newsletter

Join Persephone's Reader Group

Persephone's Playground

Follow Persephone Online

instagram.com/persephoneautumn

facebook.com/persephoneautumnwrites

tiktok.com/@persephoneautumn

goodreads.com/persephoneautumn

bookbub.com/authors/persephone-autumn

amazon.com/author/persephoneautumn

pinterest.com/persephoneautumn

twitter.com/PersephoneAutum

ACKNOWLEDGMENTS

Cracks knuckles Here we go!

To my family and friends... Thank you for your endless support and love. I wouldn't be where I am without you.

To Ellie and Rosa... Best. Editing. Team. Ever! Thanks for always correcting my punctuation (commas suck) and knowing when to use lay or lie. And thank you for the love and commentary and constructive criticism. True badasses!

To Abigail Davies... Thank you for this gorgeous cover!! Thank you for being a friend from early on and seeing my vision when I came to you with Broken Sky. I can't wait to see the rest of the series!

To all my author peeps... I love you! And we'll get there, hell or high water!

To all the readers and bloggers... Tons of hugs and a million thank yous! No words extend how much I appreciate you!

ABOUT THE AUTHOR

Persephone Autumn lives in Florida with her wife, crazy dog, and two lover-boy cats. A proud mom with a cuckoo grandpup. An ethnic food enthusiast who has fun discovering ways to veganize her favorite non-vegan foods. If given the opportunity, she would intentionally get lost in nature.

For years, Persephone did some form of writing; mostly journaling or poetry. After pairing her poetry with images and posting them online, she began the journey of writing her first novel.

She mainly writes romance, but on occasion dips her toes in other works. Look for her poetry publications and a psychological horror under P. Autumn.

9 781951 477356